I0456781

CASSIE MINT

Wild Obsession

BLACK CHERRY
PUBLISHING

Contents

Keep in touch with Cassie!   vi

I   Mountain Captive

Description   3
Natalia   4
Carver   10
Natalia   14
Carver   20
Natalia   25
Carver   31
Natalia   39
Carver   46
Natalia   50
Carver   57

II   Desert Target

Description   63
Leif   65
Hannah   70
Leif   74
Hannah   79
Leif   84

Hannah	88
Leif	94
Hannah	99
Leif	106
Hannah	110
Leif	114
Hannah	121
Leif	125
Hannah	128

III   Ocean Jewel

Description	133
Roxy	135
Damian	140
Roxy	144
Damian	150
Roxy	158
Damian	164
Roxy	169
Damian	177
Roxy	185
Damian	190

IV   Arctic Star

Description	195
Harlow	197
Cole	203
Harlow	208
Cole	215

Harlow   222
Cole   229
Harlow   236
Cole   243

Author's Note   246
About the Author   247

Keep in touch with Cassie!

Want to stay up to date with new releases, sales, and more instalove goodness?

Sign up for Cassie's newsletter!

I

Mountain Captive

Description

The Volkovs took everything from me. They destroyed my family when I was a boy.

So when the pretty little Volkov heiress stumbles past my cabin in the mountains, I can't believe my eyes.

She's sweet. Innocent. Her father should know better than to let her roam the mountains unprotected.

There are beasts out here in the wild.

Beasts and wicked men.

And none of them worse than me.

Natalia

I stumble along the forest path, trees stretching high overhead on both sides. My hiking boots are stiff, the leather new and unbroken, and there's a blister rubbed raw on my heel that stings with every step. My legs burn, my shoulders ache beneath my heavy backpack, and my lungs scream for oxygen in the thin air.

It's *amazing.* I feel so alive.

Out here, away from the constant buzz of people and cars and electronics, I'm hearing things I never really noticed before in the city. The whisper of the breeze in the leaves; the strange cries and screeches of the birds. Distant shuffling in the undergrowth. The snap of twigs and the burble of far-off water.

I don't think I've ever been left alone for more than a few hours in my whole life. Certainly not outside in the wilderness. At home, when I want a simple walk in the park, two of my father's men have to escort me.

A pang of guilt echoes through me, and I swallow hard. My

parents would be so angry if they knew I was here. Not on the heavily supervised class trip like I promised, but on a solo hike through the mountains. Far from my college professors' watchful eyes and the safety of the other students.

I'm not sorry for lying. Well, okay—I am a bit. It doesn't come naturally.

But it's the only way I could take this for myself. Two whole weeks, all on my own. Two weeks of *freedom.*

And my father has not been a reasonable man recently. For the last few months, he's been angry and vicious, prowling the halls of our family estate like a wounded animal. Any time I tried to speak to him, he lashed out, his words crackling with violence, sending me scurrying back down the halls to the safety of my bedroom.

In those moments, I wished more than ever that he'd let me live in the college dorms. But no—the daughter of the Volkov empire does not get a normal life. Does not get to choose her own destiny.

I try not to be ungrateful, but sometimes I want to scream and rake my fingernails down the walls.

No. There's no way I could have asked my father about this trip. He's been too stressed, too moody. But I also couldn't let this opportunity pass me by: a spring break where I've finally been left to make my own plans, an afterthought compared to my parents' business worries. Someone's been causing them trouble—some dark, distant figure sabotaging their every move. Cutting off contacts and spoiling deals; undercutting offers and tipping off the FBI about my father's shadiest operations.

My parents have been furious. Snarling at each other as their net worth swirls away down the drain. I've been the last thing on their minds.

I don't mind. It's a relief. I've been waiting for this taste of freedom for my entire life.

The mountains weren't an obvious choice, even to me. I'm a girly girl, with painted nails and a weakness for expensive hair products. Bugs make me squeal, and before I left on this secret trip, I'd never even *seen* a tent in person.

But what better way to test myself? To feel *true* freedom than alone, vulnerable and defiant, out here in the mountains?

It will be okay. I'm not attempting any crazy hikes or dangerous routes. Just taking in the scenery, feeling my leg muscles burn, and trying to keep myself alive. Cooking my own food; carrying my own pack. There are even cabins beside the mountain path sometimes, with the scent of wood smoke lingering in the air. I stumble past one now, sweeping my dark blonde hair out of my face so I can peer at the shadowed windows.

There's no movement inside. No signs of life—except the faint smell of cooked bacon, no doubt from breakfast a few hours ago. So you see, if I *really* got in trouble, I could find my way back to one of these cabins and knock on the rough wood door. Bring out one of the silent, sturdy men who make their homes in the mountains and beg for help.

The thought renews my confidence. I straighten my back and push down my shoulders, striding faster down the path.

I won't be knocking on anyone's door.

I'm going to finish this trip all by myself.

* * *

I set up my tiny camp when the sun sinks towards the horizon. I got caught out on my first night, bumping and fumbling around trying to set up my tent in the dark, my breath freezing in my chest when I heard animals moving nearby.

Nope. Nuh-huh. I'm not doing that again. When the last light drains from the sky, I want to be tucked up nice and cozy in my tent, feeling the day's tiredness weigh down my limbs. Sometimes I read a few chapters of my book by flashlight, or scribble a journal entry into my notebook.

Mostly, I crash. All this fresh air knocks the stuffing out of me.

I pick a pretty spot on the side of a stream. Not too close—I learned that the hard way, when the bugs ate me alive. No—I set myself up a little ways back, close enough for the pretty view and the soothing gurgle of water, but away from the clouds of mountain bugs.

My backpack crashes to the hard dirt and I let out a groan, rubbing the sore spots on my shoulders. I tilt my head this way and that, twisting my spine until my back pops, and I freeze when I twig snaps nearby.

I don't move. I barely breathe. I stand completely still, and listen.

There's no huffing of a bear. No birdsong. No sounds at all. The hairs rise on the back of my neck, and I turn on the spot, peering into the trees all around me. In all directions, there's nothing but forest and rock.

I'm alone.

Alone.

Probably.

If there's one thing I've learned as the youngest Volkov daughter, it's that bad people do bad things all the time. People are capable of horrors that most normal people can't even think of, and they do them without a flicker of guilt.

I've seen my own father in action.

So maybe it's paranoia. Maybe it's foolish to keep walking as the light dies. But my gut tells me there's something here in these trees—something watching me. Something bad. Something that wants to do me wrong.

I scoop my backpack off the dirt and heave it back onto my shoulders. Then I turn away from the stream and keep walking.

My heart pounds as I follow the dirt path, but not from the exercise this time. My breath comes in short pants, but I strain to listen for the sounds of someone following. There's nothing—no snapping twigs or heavy footsteps—and after twenty minutes of stumbling through the dying light, I find a clearing. It's small—just a gap in the trees—but there's a boulder in the center.

Perfect.

I pitch my tent quickly, as close to the boulder as I can manage. I face the door towards the trees, and for the first night of the trip, I don't make a fire or try to cook. Even though my stomach growls with hunger as I work, I pitch my tent as fast as I can then shove my backpack straight inside and crawl in after it.

I sit cross-legged in the mouth of the tent, shoving handfuls of trail mix into my mouth, and peer into the trees. That shivery feeling of being watched—it's still here.

There are eyes on me in these mountains.

Unfriendly eyes.

For the first time since I began my secret trip, I regret this decision. No one knows that I'm here. If they did, they would have stopped me, and I couldn't risk that. But now, with a dark presence following me through the trees, I'm suddenly so alone and vulnerable my stomach swoops.

I wrap the trail mix tight and stuff it in my food bag, too queasy to eat any more. I should hang it from a branch far away, to keep away the bears, but somehow when I weigh the risk of a hungry bear against the malevolent shadow in the trees...

I'm not leaving this tent.

I zip the door closed and shuffle back as far as I can, clutching my heavy flashlight in my hands.

Carver

She knows I'm here. Clever little princess. The first time I saw her tripping past my cabin like some lost city girl, I thought I was hallucinating. I've spent months, *years*, staring at surveillance photos of her and the rest of the Volkov family. At secret shots taken of her in her college classes; walking in the park with the family lackeys; through her bedroom window as she tugged a sweater over her head.

Maybe I stared at her photos more than the others. It doesn't change anything. She's still one of *them*.

The family who took everything from me.

I thought she was a figment of my imagination. A sign I'd been out here in the mountains alone too long, obsessing over my revenge plans. But when I ducked out of my back door and followed her on silent feet, I got another look at her.

I'm not insane. She really is *here*, the girl I'd planned to ruin along with the rest of the Volkovs. Wandering into my mountains like some lost little lamb. And she *must* be lost, with her overstuffed backpack tilting on her slender shoulders, and her brand new hiking boots scuffing through the dirt. I know with one glance that they're rubbing her heel.

It's too good to pass up, this opportunity. I've been making the Volkovs hurt for months, sabotaging their businesses and cutting off their ties one by one. But I never dreamed of *this*—that I'd get the Volkov girl in my clutches. At my mercy, just me and her. My cock swells unbidden at the thought, and I palm it as I follow her, weaving behind her through the trees.

It's fate.

She's so small. Delicate. Her lithe grace is clear in every light step she takes on the dirt path. And when she glances around, eyes wide and lips parted in fear, a vice constricts around my chest.

I want those eyes on me. So much I have to fight every instinct, forcing myself to stay hidden in the shadows and not step out onto the path and wave at her.

She'd only run. And then I'd have to give chase, and *fuck*, I've never been so hard in my life at that thought. At pursuing her like an animal as she crashes through the undergrowth, her eyes bright with fear...

My fevered imagination runs out there. Because when I catch her, despite the bitterness that's soaked deep into my soul, I want her willing. Fighting me, yes, thrashing and grunting, but with the same dark excitement that grips me now. I want her wet and ready and desperate for me to take her, and... fuck.

This means nothing.

It's a moment's weakness, a physical reaction to the way her hair tumbles down her back and her ass jiggles in those leggings. It's not *her*—she is a Volkov. Part of the family that destroyed me.

And she will pay.

* * *

She pitches her tent in a clearing, flush up against a boulder. It's a smart move—she's harder to sneak up on this way, and I know from the quick, harsh breaths inside the tent that she's not sleeping. She's too wary. Too afraid. I climb the boulder in slow, silent motions, pulling myself up and over the rock with languid power. And when I crouch above her tent, close and quiet enough to hear her frightened breathing, I've never felt so alive.

Primed and poised. As attuned to her as the mountain lions are to their prey. This is the most intimate experience of my life, and I haven't even looked her in the eyes. I hover above her, the mountain breeze tugging my hair back from my forehead, and consider my options.

I could speak. Break the silence. Say just her name in a low caress, and wait for her to lunge out of the tent into the clearing in a panicked haze.

Or I could drop onto the tent from above. Tear the fabric open with my bare hands and carry her kicking and screaming back to my cabin.

Or I could befriend her. 'Accidentally' meet her tomorrow in the light of day, when her guard is down and she's ready to trust again. Play the friendly local guide, and lure her back to my cabin willingly.

The options swirl and catch in my brain, each of them tempting me one by one. They all offer unique potential. But as I mull over my choices, her breathing softens and slows beneath me in the tent, until finally she slips into sleep. Her deep, heavy breaths mingle with the rustling and scurrying of the forest, and I find myself lingering just to listen to her.

She's not what I pictured.

Out here, unprotected. Her eyes shining bright with unbridled joy as she soaks in the beauty of the mountains. And that vulnerable hitch in her breath when she sensed she was being followed...

She's no mobster's ice princess.

Natalia Volkova is something else. Something *more.*

She's a puzzle to solve. A question to answer. And I will solve her—as I use her for revenge.

Natalia

∽⟋ᴑᴑ⟍∽

I wake as a strong arm slides beneath my back. For a crazy, sleep-muddled moment, I'm a little girl again and my father is carrying me upstairs to bed, cradled against his chest. I hum and burrow closer, pressing my face against the hot skin of his throat, and the sleeping bag whispers as it twists around me.

The sleeping bag.

Oh god.

I suck in a sharp breath, wrenching my body away. I kick and thrash and fight, but I'm trapped by my own freaking sleeping bag, and the man inside my tent is strong and calm. He moves with firm deliberation, knotting a strip of fabric between my teeth, muffling my cries, and lashing my arms to my sides through the slippery fabric.

He speaks as he works in a low, soothing tone, like I'm a wild animal trapped in a snare. I gnaw at the fabric gag, tossing my head to the side and catching him on the jaw. He curses and rocks back on his heels, a dark shape in the cramped tent, and hot tears slide down my cheeks into my hair. Wrenching

14

sobs shake my chest as he lunges forward again, picking me up easily and bundling out into the night air.

No. No. No.

I shake my head, wriggling and writhing in his grip, and he speaks low and urgent in my ear.

"Be still. *Still,* princess. I'm not going to hurt you."

As if I'd believe a word this man said. I scream harder against the gag, tearing my throat, and I can taste the coppery tang of fear on the back of my tongue. I throw all my weight to one side, taking him off guard, and I wrench out of his arms onto the dirt.

Hitting the ground steals my breath, but I'm already wriggling away, kicking at the sleeping bag tangled around my legs. The man curses loudly, gathering me back into his arms like I weigh less than a twig. Like all my fight, all my strength, is a nuisance and nothing more.

I'm caught.

I slump against his hard body, my chest aching from crying, panic weighing my limbs down like lead weights. My pulse thrums beneath my jaw, tapping against the skin.

"That's better." His fingers sift through my hair. "I won't hurt you, princess. I promise. We'll send a quick message to your father and then it will all be over."

… Over?

My father?

Cold dread slides down my spine.

This man knows who I am. Who my father is.

And he means to kill me.

* * *

15

My captor lives in the cabin I walked past this morning. He carries me there through the forest with absurd gentleness, cradled against his chest like a bride, and when he pushes the door open and carries me over the threshold, I squeeze my eyes shut tight.

Light flares in the cabin. It tints my eyelids pink, and I don't fight anymore as he pauses in the center of the floor, then carries me to one corner.

He lays me down, slow and careful, a mattress creaking beneath my weight. My eyes snap open, the fight flooding back to my limbs, but he's already digging my hands out of the sleeping bag and lashing them to the bed rail with the rope he used earlier. It's one of the tent's guy-lines, I realize dimly. He didn't even need equipment to abduct me. He just *took* me. Like a penny off the sidewalk.

"It's alright, princess."

I glare at him through narrowed eyes as he steps back from the bed, rubbing a hand over his jaw. His eyes rake over the length of my body, naked hunger in their dark depths, but even though my core pulses hot with anticipation, he doesn't move to touch me again.

He just watches, his face in shadow.

His breath drags in and out of his lungs.

Then he turns on his heel and strides away, rummaging through the desk propped against the opposite wall. I take the chance to stare around my surroundings, looking for anything—a weapon. A clue to my captor's identity. A kernel of hope.

Anything.

The cabin is larger than it seemed from outside. I'm stretched out and tied to a double bed with a charcoal gray bedspread, and a simple woven rug covers the floorboards. There's a simple kitchen range in one corner of the single room; a wood-burner and lumpy sofa in the other. The man bends over a desk piled high with books and papers and gadgets, and I realize belatedly that the red lights of electronics blink at me from around the cabin.

At the back of the desk, two large monitors are dark. A computer whirs quietly beneath the table, and pinned to a cork board on the wall are photos. Dozens, no, *hundreds* of photos, taken from behind bushes and around corners.

Surveillance photos.

Of my family.

Photos of *me*.

The man straightens, something gripped in one hand, and I shrink back against the mattress as he comes closer. But he stops several paces away, scowling down at the camera in his hand. The lamplight washes across half his face, and I can see him a little better now.

He's...

God.

He's not what I expected.

His skin is warm golden brown—flushed with the deep, healthy tan of an outdoorsman. His shoulders are broad and sculpted, his chest toned beneath his blue flannel shirt, and pale scars fleck his corded forearms. His face is etched with bitterness, but there's something else in his brown eyes when he looks at me.

Sorrow, maybe. Regret.

"A few photos, princess," he rasps. "To send to your father."

I shake my head, tugging frantically against the rope around my wrists, but he doesn't hurt me like I expect. Doesn't touch me at all. He snaps three quick photos, taking different angles, a frown creasing his forehead. Then he nods and turns away, striding back to the desk and booting his computer to life. The monitors flick on but he kills them quickly, before I can see anything on the screens. And he keeps talking to me in that low rumbling, like he can't help but tell me things. Can't help but confess his sins.

"They'll be untraceable. He won't know where to look for you."

For my body? I wrench harder against the ropes.

"This is… unpleasant for both of us." I roll my eyes, still wet with tears. *Poor sad kidnapper.* And he must see me, because he grates out a laugh. "It will be over soon, princess. We'll torment your father for a few days, leverage this carefully, and then you'll go free. You have my word."

We?

He's talking like we're in this together somehow. Like we're both victims in this scenario. But *I* am the girl with a gag between her teeth, and he is the man striding freely around his cabin, lighting a fire in the wood burner and putting on water to boil. He flicks glances at me as he works, and every time is like a physical touch.

I can't help myself. I don't even realize I'm doing it. I arch under his gaze, twisting to show him the length of me, my skin heating under his perusal. His eyes darken, but he looks away.

A strange disappointment sinks through my gut.

"I told you, princess. I won't hurt you. I gave you my word."

He crosses back to the desk, tapping on the keyboard, and photos of me fill the monitors. I look *wrecked*—red faced and snotty, hair wild and cheeks wet. The gag cuts harshly across my face, and my arms are wrenched awkwardly over my head.

Heat pulses again between my thighs, and I tear my eyes away to glare at the ceiling.

I won't help this man. I won't trust him. My traitorous body can respond to him all it likes—it changes nothing.

And the second I get free, I will kill him.

Carver

The Volkov princess is plotting against me. Who can blame her? I'd do exactly the same thing. I *am* doing the same thing—that's how we both found ourselves here. She may not know it yet, but we have a lot in common.

We both have a thirst for revenge.

Her eyes dart around my cabin, cataloguing her surroundings. She's been here for several hours now, but she shows no sign of tiring. Her gaze keeps drifting back to the same things: the poker beside the fire; the knife block in the kitchen; the photos of her pinned to my cork board. Seeing it now with fresh eyes, I can understand the raw fear freezing her features—there are five photos of her for every one of someone else. Though her father has always been my main target for revenge, she's become a separate obsession.

It's the gold flecks in her hazel eyes. The delicate purse of her lips. The soft smile that plays over her mouth when she reads her favorite books.

I glance over at her flushed, angry face.

I will never see that smile. Not directed at *me.* And it's ridiculous to feel such deep sorrow at that—to feel such painful loss that it's like I'm in mourning.

A thought strikes me, hot and sudden.

If she weren't Natalia Volkova, tied to her poisonous family, I would *want* her. Not just for a date or a single night, but with an all-consuming hunger. To claim her, to spoil her, to *possess* her. It prowls inside me now as I watch her, soaking in the sight of her draped over my bed. Her hair splays over *my* pillow; her scent mingles with mine in the sheets. And her wrists...

It makes me a monster and I know it, but I love the sight of her tied.

Her breath hitches and I look back at her face. She's watching me, chest heaving beneath the twisted sleeping bag, but her pupils are so dilated her eyes are nearly black.

Fuck. Little Natalia likes this too.

Oh, her fear is real. The violence she promises me with every glance—that is real. But so is the arousal which wets her lips and makes her squirm like that on my mattress. She tugs again at the rope, but not like she wants to escape.

Like she's testing the bond. Relishing the sensation of being caught.

Caught by me.

A muffled groan sounds behind the strip of fabric between her teeth. My cock pulses, growing hard in response. I rub a hand over my jaw, then step closer.

She freezes as I approach the bed. Her eyes gaze up at me as I tower above her.

"Are you needy, Natalia?" My voice rumbles through the quiet cabin. "Are you aching between your legs?"

21

I wait, pulse thrumming, as her eyes widen. Then finally, *finally*, she tips her chin in a tiny nod.

"Do you want me to fix that for you?" I rasp. Behind my back, I clench my fists so tight my knuckles creak.

She watches me for what feels like an age, her eyes darting to the cabin walls and then back. Her breaths come quick and shallow, the movement dipping the sleeping bag. I'm about to turn away, to take her silence as refusal, but she makes a small, urgent sound.

She nods once, short and firm.

Hunger roars through my chest.

* * *

This wasn't part of the plan. I never intended to *touch* her. To feel myself slipping deeper and deeper into her thrall. But when I step close to the bed, leaning down to drag the sleeping bag zipper open, suddenly *I* am the one who is trapped.

The smooth skin beneath her vest top. The perky mounds of her tits. The points of her nipples prodding the fabric.

I'm lost, I'm fucking drowning in her, and I can't help but duck my head and breathe in the scent of her neck. She makes a muffled noise, but she doesn't squirm away. If anything, she tilts her head to give me better access.

And god, she smells good. Like the wind through the leaves, like mountain springs, and the faint musk of sweat that comes from hiking for hours each day. It's the most delicious thing I've ever smelled, and I want to lick her from head to toe. I want to rub my face in her bare stomach.

I grit my teeth and straighten up. Wait until she meets my eye.

"Are you sure?"

A nod.

"You want me to touch you? Touch your pussy? Final warning."

She rolls her eyes. Nods again. And she can pretend to be distant and unaffected, but she's squirming below me, pressing her thighs together. Looking for the friction she needs.

I can give that to her.

"This changes nothing," I tell her, tugging the sleeping bag down her body. She lifts her hips to help. "I'm still going to ruin your father."

She glares at me but doesn't shake her head. Doesn't tell me to stop. No; the second the sleeping bag frees her feet, she spreads her thighs wide. Her hiking socks are bunched around her ankles, and dried dirt crusts one knee.

"Now there's a sight." I scrub a hand down my throat. A drumbeat starts in my chest. There's a damp patch shadowed on the seam of her leggings. It's warm beneath the pads of my fingers as I ghost them over the fabric.

Soft. Teasing. Feather-light touches meant to drive her as insane as she's made me feel. She turns me on so much that I'm vicious with it, a wounded animal, and I want to share that pain around.

Let her see how it feels.

Natalia whimpers, lifting her hips to chase my touch. I draw my hand back with a dark chuckle.

"Oh, no. That's not how this works, princess. You're at my mercy. I'm going to torment you, deny you the way you've never been denied in your whole spoiled life, and when I finally let you come, you'll beg for relief."

She watches me, eyes glassy as I sit beside her. The mattress dips under my weight and she rolls against my hip. She doesn't try to move away. I'm talking a big game, spilling the words I *know* will make her wet, but the truth is I'm so hard my teeth ache.

It's a battle. A test of my will. Every atom of me screams to just *take* her. To cover her body with my own; to press her down into the creaky bed springs; to fuck and taste and bite.

But despite her family name, I can't bring myself to hate her. Not for a moment since I laid eyes on her in the forest. And maybe I'm delusional, but I want her to crave me the same way.

So I'll make it good for her. I'll make her weep tears of frustration, of pent up need, and then sweet, sweet relief.

And when I send the Volkov princess back home, she'll never forget the man in the mountains.

Natalia

⟨❧⟩

If my body weren't singing with scrapes and bruises, I'd think this was a dream. The kind I have sometimes on slow summer nights when my bedroom is too warm and I prop the window open for a breeze. When I sleep on top of the bed covers with only a thin sheet pulled to my waist, and my nipples harden beneath every brush of my camisole over my skin.

A good dream.

A gooey, aching dream.

Except if *I* were driving this fantasy, my kidnapper wouldn't tease me so badly. Everything else he's done tonight, he's done with ruthless efficiency. Quick and deft and then done. But this, he takes his goddamn time. It's enough to make me slam my head back against the pillow.

He unwraps me like the most delicate of gifts. Which sounds lovely, but is really a drawn-out torture of fingertips brushing over my heated skin. He peels my clothes off one piece at a time, moving slower than dripping honey. His movements are cruelly tender, and when he finally cups my hip bone in

25

his palm, my stomach muscles are shuddering with desire. I rock to the side, pressing into his touch, and finally, *finally*, he squeezes me. He kneads the swell of my hip, scowling at the curves of my body like they're a personal insult to him.

I might be self-conscious. I might want to cover up, feeling unattractive. But it's so crystal clear that he wants me badly, that he's *furious* about it, and instead I stretch and preen like a smug house cat under his intense gaze.

Look, I want to tell him. *Look at the trap you've made for yourself.*

He wants me. He won't—he *can't* hurt me.

I know that now. And I can use it against him.

"Stop it." He shakes my hip, but I wriggle closer, pressing against him. He blows out a shaky sigh, dropping his chin and muttering something under his breath, and all the while his fingers are kneading me. Rubbing burning circles into my skin. I'm soaking wet between my legs, throbbing and pulsing down there in ways I've never felt before, but he's undone too.

He jerks his head up, a hard glint in his eye.

"Is that how we're playing this, princess? A battle of wills?"

I turn my head and run the tip of my nose up his forearm.

He curses darkly, lurching off the bed, and stands over me, chest heaving. I spread my legs wider, only flushing slightly darker at my bareness, and glare at him in challenge.

No one has ever laid eyes on me there. My most secret parts. And now the first man to see all of me is a rough stranger in the mountains—a man who stole me away in the night and lashed me to his bedpost. But I am truly my father's daughter, wicked and wild, because the thought only makes my pussy flood wetter.

"You're soaked, Natalia." He traces a circle onto my ankle

bone, then draws a line up the inside of my calf. "I can see it from here. You're *glistening*."

His finger reaches the inside of my knee, lingering for a second before swooping up my thigh. It's so ticklish, so sensitive, that I actually huff a laugh around the gag. His mouth twitches, but his face smooths back to careful blankness.

"Has anyone ever touched you here before?"

I have. If he hadn't gagged me, I'd tell him so. I'd tell him all of it. But he did gag me, so he doesn't get to know those things. I simply shake my head. And something warms in my chest when relief flits through his expression.

"Good," he rasps. "Good girl."

Oh. When he calls me that, my pussy clenches down on nothing, on the horrible emptiness that I've never noticed before. It makes the ticklish feeling down there worse, and a faint sound escapes around the gag. It's wounded and desperate, and a cruel smirk plays over the man's face before he relents and slides his finger along my slit.

"So wet." His voice is ragged. "So eager for me, princess."

I wish I could argue. Could proclaim that it's *not* for him. But that would be a lie, wouldn't it? It's all for him. Every drop and whimper; every crackle of sensation on my oversensitive skin.

I'm open and ready and waiting for him. And suddenly, I want more than his touch.

I want *all* of him.

This time, I'm glad for the gag. It saves me from myself. From my twisted desires. And I bite down on the fabric, musty and rough in my mouth, as his broad fingertips play through my folds. He's relaxed, exploratory, not trying to ease my ache. Not yet.

Not until I weep with frustration.

I've wept so many tears for this man already tonight. Tears of shock, of fear, of fury.

These are tears I will be glad to weep.

"Fuck," he mutters, and I'm so relieved to hear the rough edge to his voice. He's coming undone too, his calm exterior cracking, the strain showing in the set of his shoulders and the muscle ticking in his jaw. He moves his fingers with more purpose, dipping just slightly into my center before sweeping up to my clit. He traces circles around it, light then firm then light again, and I pant against the gag, kicking my legs as my muscles twitch.

"Easy," he murmurs, working me faster, and I growl into the fabric. I lift my hips, trying to urge him on, to take him inside me, but he's true to his word. His fingers dance out of reach, always teasing, never bringing relief, and the constant, unrelenting onslaught of sensations winds me tighter and tighter. I'm coiled and trembling, stomach muscles shuddering as sweat dampens the backs of my knees. Still, he taunts and teases me, until I scream in frustration against the gag.

"*There.*" He flicks the pad of his thumb over my clit, bearing down with the pressure I need. My hips thrust off the mattress as an orgasm rolls through me, fierce and somehow sharp. It scratches the itch he's set under my skin, but *barely*, and I'm still so on edge that my jaw aches from clenching my teeth. I collapse back onto the bed as the last waves pass through me, and I scowl up at him weakly.

"Not enough?" His mouth quirks with amusement. I shake my head once, hard. He *knows*. The bastard knows what he's doing to me. "Poor needy princess. With *such* an aching cunt."

His words should shock me. Should rile me up and make

28

me hate him. But instead they soak through me like sunshine, and I sigh and preen.

"*Fuck.*"

The creak of the bed springs is my only warning.

The man leans one knee on the foot of the bed and slides both hands under my ass cheeks. He lifts me easily, bringing my pussy to his face as I squawk and slide down the mattress.

His first lick is long. Hard. A broad swipe of his tongue. And the groan that shudders out of him rattles all the way down to my bones.

My kidnapper eats my pussy like a starving man. Like he's on death row and this is his last meal. There's no part of me that he doesn't lick and suck and nibble, and there's no finesse in his movements. He's too hungry. Too desperate.

I shudder and cry out against the fabric between my teeth, thrashing as I fight to get closer to him, the bed rail creaking as I tug on my ties. Finally, I lock my thighs around his neck and *squeeze*, holding him there, forcing his tongue deeper inside me. The metal bed rail thunks to the side but we keep going, keep moaning, and I only realize that one wrist has come free when my fingers wrap around the metal rail of their own accord.

My breath catches. I force my wrist back into place, trying to think straight as I hover on the edge of oblivion.

"Oh no, you don't," he growls into my slick flesh. "Don't deny me, Natalia."

A single crack of his palm against my ass sends me toppling over, spiraling down and down and down until pleasure sings through my nerves and my body stiffens in his arms. He cradles me like something precious as I shudder and gasp, licking me steadily until I'm done.

He lays me gently on the bedspread. When he lifts his head,

his chin shines slick in the lamplight. There's something in his expression—something like awe, something like regret—but then he blinks and it's gone.

"Sleep well, princess." He pushes to his feet and leaves the cabin, the door slamming shut behind him.

I wriggle my newly freed fingers. He never rechecked my ties.

Carver

The night is loud in the mountains. An endless ghostly chorus of hooting owls, of snuffling bears in the distance, of cracking twigs and the wind moaning through the trees. I stand on the deck of my cabin and breathe it all in, trying and failing to get my head on straight.

This is wrong. It's slipping away from me. I swore not to touch her, and then...

I hang my head, gripping the wooden rail. It doesn't matter that she wanted it. I'm losing control of the situation. How can I use her for vengeance while she consumes me, body and soul? Even now, I want her so badly it's a sickness. I want to sink my cock deep inside her, yes, but I want to sit near her, too. Listen to her breathing. Play with the ends of her hair. The reason I took her at all, my need for revenge against her father—it's fading away. Getting lost in the background.

No.

I straighten my shoulders. I will not be distracted from my purpose. The Volkovs destroyed my family, and they will pay.

I'll shelter Natalia from the worst of it, if I can, but I won't be swayed from my path.

Her father will know the same horror and grief that he made *us* feel.

The wooden boards creak as I stride back across the deck, pushing back into the cabin. It's warmer in here, the smell of sex lingering in the air, and Natalia watches me with cunning eyes. She's debauched, her cheeks flushed and her hair tangled on the pillow, but still she grunts and squeezes her thighs together when she sees me. I've teased her too well.

"More?"

Her eyes narrow. It's not an outright yes, so she'll go without. I stride to the desk, bending over the monitors. There's a reply from her father already, a senseless stream of threats, but it's clear that he hasn't been able to trace us.

Good. The manic edge to his messages makes me smirk.

Let him suffer.

Natalia shifts behind me on the bed, but I push it from my mind. This constant awareness of her is a weakness. It's not the awareness of an opponent, but an endless craving to get my hands on her again. She's the worst kind of distraction, and I force myself to ignore the creaks and huffed breaths coming from the bed.

I should have known better. I underestimated this young woman, but she is a Volkov after all. I don't even register the long silence until she's pressed against my back, the edge of a knife digging into my throat.

One of *my* knives. From the kitchen block. Has she been roaming around behind me while I forcibly ignore her? A bizarre rush of pride fills me—she's perfect, a vicious treasure—but she digs the blade deeper into my skin. A bead of blood wells up and trickles down from the cut.

"What's the plan, Natalia?" I murmur. "Are you going to slit my throat?"

"You deserve it," she croaks, and it's the first time I've heard her voice. Her words are rough from screaming and moaning for half the night, but I can still hear the musical tone.

God. She's going to kill me, and I'll die with a smile on my face. I'm wrecked.

"Let me go."

I chuckle. "Back into the forest? Are you going to find your tent and pretend none of this happened?"

She pauses. Huffs in annoyance. Then: "Fine. I'll kill you and use your computers to call for help."

She could do that. It's a solid plan, and I'm pleased that she came up with it under all this stress. When I turn around to face her, the blade slices deeper through my skin, and she gasps as she sees the line of red, but her grip doesn't falter.

"I'm sorry, princess." I catch her wrist and *squeeze*, grinding the bones, and she yelps and drops the knife. That sound of her pain is like a blow to my chest, and I cradle her poor wrist as she snuffles, tugging against my hold.

"Wait a moment. Let me check for damage."

She chokes out a laugh. "You should look in the mirror."

There's the slightest accent to her voice. It's the sexiest thing I've ever heard. Her wrist is fine, just pink and tender, and I guide her gently to the kitchen, placing her far from the knife block as I rummage in the chest freezer. I wrap a heavy bag of frozen peas in a dish cloth and place it on her wrist, catching her other hand to hold it there.

She watches me warily, peas pressed to her wrist as I dig through the drawers for painkillers and fill a glass in the sink.

"Here." I hold out two aspirin, but her hands are both busy. She lifts an eyebrow and presents her tongue. My cock pulses as I place the pills on her little pink tongue, lifting the glass to her lips so she can take a sip.

"Wait," she rasps as I turn to place it on the counter. She unwraps the dish cloth and runs it under the faucet. When she reaches up and dabs at the cut on my throat, I turn to stone under her careful hands.

Perhaps this is it. A distraction before she sinks another hidden knife deep into my gut.

It's worth the risk.

But she swabs at me gently, grumbling when the blood doesn't come away easily.

"Leave it. I'll wash it off in the shower."

She lights up at those words, her gaze darting around the cabin, and I can see the hope brewing in her tired eyes. She's been hiking for days. Trussed up in that sleeping bag all night. Then made sticky and sweaty as I coaxed her to come twice on my fingers and tongue.

Am I really going to do this? Let the girl I kidnapped take a hot shower, like this is some hotel and not the site of my vengeance?

She blinks up at me, teeth digging into her plump bottom lip.

Fuck.

I am.

* * *

"What's your name?"

The shower spray drums against the tiles, steam curling around us. I couldn't leave her in here unsupervised—not with the razor and the toothbrush and a dozen other things she could attack me with—but I couldn't tell her no either.

I have a sinking feeling that I'll never tell her no again.

"Carver."

She hums. "Carver what?"

"Carver Ennox." I wait, but there's no sign of recognition. I guess the Volkovs ruin so many lives, it must be hard to keep the names straight.

"Are you going to kill me, Carver?"

I tense. "Why do you ask that?" I've promised not to hurt her so many times tonight.

"Why else would you risk telling me your name?"

I gust out a breath. She's got me there. "Maybe I'm just tired. And you're too clever for me. I keep letting my guard down."

Natalia spins under the hot spray, sighing as it beats against her sore shoulders. From here, leaning back against the wall, I can see every scrape and cut and bruise on her body.

Did I put any of those there?

God, I hope not.

"So when I tell the FBI that a man named Carver Ennox kidnapped me..."

"I suppose they'll come to arrest me."

I won't put up a fight. By then, I'll have had my revenge, and I'll be ready to go peacefully.

"Will you visit me in prison?" I ask suddenly.

She laughs at me, full of wicked delight. "Maybe. Will you still want to see me if I get you arrested?"

That's an easy one. "Yes."

Natalia grins, eyes warm, and I press my palms flat against the wall to keep from going over there and joining her. She notices, her gaze heating, then turns her back to me. She sways her hips side to side as she showers, taunting me the way I teased her. Her ripe, round ass is perfect, begging to be spanked, and her throaty laugh makes me jerk.

"Do you want to join me?"

"No." I don't trust myself not to touch her. Not to slam her up against the tiles and fuck her tight pussy until she screams.

Natalia pouts. "Why not?"

I shrug, noncommittal. It pisses her off even worse, and she glares over her shoulder as she places her palms on the tiles and tilts her ass up for me.

"Are you sure about that, Carver?"

I scrub a hand over my jaw, watching her with clenched teeth. Rivulets of hot water stream over her flushed skin, trickling over the curve of her ass, her hips, the jutting shoulder blades of her back. I could live off the water dripping off her body, licking it up bead by bead. I'd never drink from a glass again.

"I'm sure."

She huffs and drops her hands, moving back under the spray. My princess is not used to being denied.

"Well, will you help me at least?"

"Help you," I repeat flatly.

"With the shampoo."

"... The shampoo."

"Yes. *Someone* hurt my wrist." Guilt swells in my throat, choking me, and I snatch the shampoo off the shelf without another word. I don't bother to undress, yanking the shower door open and stepping inside in my boots, jeans and shirt. The water patters against my clothes, soaking them quickly and pasting them to my body. Natalia blinks at me in shock but she recovers quickly, turning and tilting back her head.

The shampoo spreads over my palm, cool compared to the steamy shower. Natalia hums as I massage it into her hair, scratching at her scalp before working it through to the ends. We stand in silence, the room quiet except for the drumming spray and Natalia's quick, shallow breaths. Her bare toes scrunch against the floor.

"You could have done this yourself."

She huffs a laugh.

"You wanted my hands on you." I push her to admit it. To admit out loud that I can't have hurt her too badly—not if she lured me in here just to touch her. But Natalia just smiles, her cheeks lifting as she faces away, and backs up half a step until her back brushes my wet shirt.

"I'm sorry about your throat," she says suddenly.

I frown at her soapy head, hands still buried in her hair. "Don't be."

"But—"

"Don't be," I clip out, even firmer. She quiets down, leaning back against my chest. And when I press my nose to the side of her throat and breathe her in, a shudder wracks the length of her body, her nipples pebbling against the misty air.

Something moves by my cock. She's moving her hips again, squirming back against me, and it takes every inch of my self control to pull my hands away and step out of the shower.

"I thought you were going to wash your cut?" She scowls at me, annoyed again. *Brat.* I stifle a smile, kicking off my soaked boots.

"I will. Once you're finished."

"What if I run while you're in there?"

I smirk, my voice dropping lower. "Then I'll chase you."

Natalia sucks in a sharp breath, her pupils blowing wide, and *fuck,* this girl will be the death of me. I promised her—promised myself—that I'd let her go free after a few days.

I'm not so sure anymore.

I'm already damned. An irredeemable sinner.

And now I want to keep her.

Natalia

It's late when we emerge from the bathroom, the door perfectly blended with the cabin walls. The night is inky black, with the kind of unreal quality that comes several hours after midnight. Everything feels like a dream, like another world, and when Carver bundles me up in his clothes, dressing me with care, I feel no fear. Only gooey warmth and a fierce longing that steals my breath.

It's twisted. So messed up. But this man speaks to my soul in a way that no one has before. I understand him better with a single glance than I do with people I've known for my whole life. And he reads me too, parsing my moods and desires as easily as though they were written on my forehead.

There's more to this. Carver wouldn't wage war on my family without reason—I *know* that. Surer than I know my own name.

"Are you going to tie me up again?" I ask as Carver kneels and tugs a pair of thick woolen socks onto my feet. With his sweatpants double knotted at my waist and a long-sleeved cotton t-shirt swamping my arms, I've never felt so cozy.

Carver's mouth twitches. He keeps his face lowered, lifting one of my feet and tugging the sock over my ankle as I lean on his shoulder for balance.

"Do you want me to?"

Mm. Yes.

I lick my lips and consider my answer. "It depends."

His eyebrow quirks. He didn't expect that. "On what, princess?"

"Why do you hate my family?"

He stills. Stares down at the floorboards, carved from stone, my ankle held forgotten in his hands. I pluck at his fresh t-shirt and he jerks back to life, placing my foot back down.

"It's complicated."

"I can keep up."

He scowls at me, pushing to his feet. Standing like this, toe to toe, he's so much taller than me. He's taller and broader and sculpted with hard muscle, and damn if that doesn't make warmth spread under my skin. Even the pissed off slant to his mouth—that heats my blood. Reminds me of the glorious stinging smack he laid on my ass a few hours ago.

Carver reads the arousal in my face. In the twin points of my nipples poking at his shirt. And for the first time since he stole me from the forest, the sight leaves him cold. He scoffs, stepping around me and crossing to his desk to fuss with the monitors. He ignores me completely, shutting me out like I'm nothing, and somehow that's the worst thing he's done to me so far. I glance at the knife block in the kitchen, fingers twitching, but he speaks without even turning around.

"Don't even think about it."

"Think about *what?*" I snarl.

He blows out a long breath and doesn't answer.

"Carver."

He taps at the keyboard. No doubt tormenting my father with more threats. He clicks away at his mouse, sifting through loose papers on the desk, and *god,* I could scream this whole cabin down. I march toward the knife block, shoulders rigid, but he curses and lunges to meet me halfway. Carver bundles me into his arms, kicking and thrashing, and the iron bands of his arms around my chest make my stomach swoop.

"Stop it," he grunts, dragging me towards the bed. Back to the metal bed rail and the rope and square freaking one. I fight him harder, true panic rising in my throat, but his jaw is set as he tosses me onto the mattress. He kneels over me, face in shadow, reaching for the rope, but I scramble back, my palms raised.

"Wait. Wait."

Carver pauses. His chest heaves up and down, the only sign that this affects him at all.

I take a deep breath. Swallow around the lump in my throat. Then rest the trembling palm of my hand on his rigid cheek.

"I just want to understand," I whisper. "I want to know why this happened to me."

He screws his eyes shut, expression pained, and I wet my lip as I wait for him to move again. To lash me to the bed rail or to kiss me or to tell all his secrets.

Something.

Anything.

Anything but this agonizing silence.

"Do you recognize the name Ennox?" I shake my head eagerly, shuffling further back on the mattress. Carver doesn't sit beside me like I want, but he does keep talking. Each word seems to pain him, like they slice him on the way out. "Well, you should. Our fathers were once closer than brothers."

I blink, shocked, but now that Carver has begun to talk, he can't seem to stop. He lets it all out in one rush: our fathers' closeness; their early businesses together; the summers Carver spent with my family before I was born. The things he tells me, the details he knows of the Volkovs—no one knows these things. It must be true. And when his face clouds over and his words turn to fractured trust, to betrayal, to my father's ruthless bid for control of their shared companies—that rings true, too.

I've always known my father is brutal. That he can be cruel. I've always been slightly afraid.

He saves the worst details for last. My father's affair with his mother; the wreckage of his parents' marriage while my own mother carried on in denial. The Volkovs decimated Carver's family, left them bankrupt and bitter and unable to spend five minutes in the same room. Carver's father turned to the bottle and his mother retreated inside her own mind, and their twelve-year-old son was left all alone with the bailiffs knocking.

And Carver swore vengeance. Swore that my father would know the same pain. I listen to his story with tears sliding down my cheeks, knowing deep in my soul that not a single word is a lie.

It's awful.

Breathtakingly cruel.

And the worst thing is, my family has left a trail of destruction ever since. If the Ennox family were early victims, in some ways they got off lightly.

The Volkovs today are ruthless. Power hungry and cold. I

was raised to be proud of that fact, but hearing this story first-hand, my heart aches and guilt curdles my gut. For twenty years, I've looked the other way. Chosen not to look too closely at my family's impact, and let my parents dictate every decision in my life. I may not have hurt Carver's family, but I'm guilty too in my own way.

"I'm sorry," I whisper, and Carver glances at me sharply. Irritation etches his features, and his eyes rake over my face, searching for a lie. Searching for a hint of disbelief.

He won't find it. I believe it all.

I wet my lip. Clear my throat. "What are you going to do with me? To get revenge."

Carver meets my eyes. "At first, I planned to hurt you." I wince, but he keeps talking, voice steady and low. "Then once I saw you, I knew that was impossible. I could never go through with it. So I planned to stage photos. To make it look like I'd tortured you."

I nod slowly. "Okay... Okay. We can do that. We can make it look real."

But Carver's already shaking his head. "No. We can't. *I* can't. I don't want those images in my brain, princess, not even faked. I can't—I can't bear it." He shudders out a sigh, rubbing his hands over his face, and he looks so defeated, so *lost,* that my chest throbs.

"I have an idea," I whisper.

Carver looks at me, eyes bleak.

"You're going to help me torment your father."

"Yes." I steel myself and shove at his shoulder. "Fetch your camera." My mind is racing, my thoughts blurring together, but I know one thing that will drive my father out of his mind. That will fill him with white-hot rage, the same rage that

Carver feels for him. The rage that stalked me, that terrified me, throughout my childhood, when my father prowled the halls of our home in his black moods.

No one needs to get hurt. Not really.

Not if we do this my way.

Carver clenches his jaw but pushes off the bed, striding to the desk and back. He hands me the camera without a word, and I pat the bed beside me as I prod at the buttons. It flickers to life and I pass Carver the camera as soon as he's settled, bare feet on the floorboards.

"What are you—"

He cuts off as I slide off the mattress, down onto my knees. I crawl between his legs, nudging his knees wider, and smooth my palms up his thighs. His navy sweatpants are soft under my hands, clinging to hard, bunched muscles.

"Princess," he rasps.

"Yes?" I breathe. My thumbs rub tiny circles over the fabric. He's so tense beneath my touch that he's practically vibrating, and my pulse drums so loud in my ears that I have to strain to hear him.

"Fuck. Natalia. *Yes.*"

I tug at the drawstring on his waistband. He lifts his hips as I work his sweatpants down, just enough to reach in and free his cock. He's half-hard, lengthening in my grip, and he watches me with burning eyes as I weigh him in my palm. He's heavy already, getting heavier by the second, and my pussy clenches at the thought of him pushing inside me. Stretching my walls. The steady, breathless *invasion* of him.

"Don't forget." I nod at the camera, and he hurries to get me in frame.

"Photos or video?"

I scratch my fingernails over his thigh, the sound rasping through the quiet cabin. The fire pops in the wood burner in the corner of the room. I hum, considering, sitting back on my heels to take in every inch of him. From his dark hair, still damp from the shower, to the broad shoulders stretching his white t-shirt, to the impressive length now rock-hard and heated in my grip.

My heart thuds in my chest, lunging against my rib cage like it's trying to batter its way through to him.

Mine.

Carver is mine.

More mine than the other Volkovs have ever been. A kindred spirit, with the same hard edges. The same soft wishes and dark desires.

I wink at him. "Kidnapper's choice."

A long breath rushes out of him, and his grin is feral as he leans back and rests on one palm.

"Smile, princess. Time to show your daddy what you think of me."

Carver

There's no way she'll go through with this. That's my first thought, when Natalia nudges my legs wider and settles on her knees between my thighs. But just the suggestion has my cock swelling, growing hard and flushed in her grip. Her hand is so small around me, her fingers delicate and pale, and my chest squeezes tight at the sight.

"Don't forget." She nods at the camera in my hand, and then her hand is moving. Her touch is gentle, absent-minded as we settle the details, and it's so distracting I can barely think straight. Doesn't she know her hand on me is the only thing I can process?

Her little pink tongue flicks out, wetting her bottom lip, and *fuck*, this can't be real.

But the tug of her warm hand—that's real.

The pinprick red glare of the camera light—that's real.

And the whisper of her damp hair over my thighs as she bends her head—that's the only sound I want to hear again. That, and her hungry groan after her first lick of my cock.

Natalia's eyes turn glassy as she takes my cock in her mouth, sucking until her cheeks hollow. She bobs her head, taking me deeper and deeper, her sweet little hums vibrating into my skin.

"Natalia. *Fuck.* That mouth, princess. You take me like such a good girl."

Her mouth quirks as she smiles as much as she can with my cock stretching her lips. She looks past the camera trained on her, trapping me in her gaze, and it's just us in this moment. Just our moans and our quick breaths and this unstoppable pull together.

She pulls off with a wet pop, resting her chin on my thigh, and smirks.

"Do you have a message for my father?" Her chest heaves up and down, brushing against my legs.

"Yes," I growl, and take a fistful of her hair. I wind it around my hand, squeezing until she gasps, then push her face back to my cock. "Carver Ennox sends his regards."

She takes me deep, eyes watering as she stares directly into the camera lens. I keep my grip on her hair tight, moving her roughly, and her cheeks flush as she moans around my cock. My princess likes it harsh, likes to be taken and treated like a plaything, and my own breaths grow ragged in response.

She wants a bad man?

I'll be that for her.

I was made to fuck Natalia Volkova.

My hips move of their own accord, snapping up towards her and thrusting me deeper, and she scrabbles to grip the bed covers but keeps going. She's magic, such a goddamn fighter, and it's her name that I groan as I yank her off. She's breathing hard, eyes dazed, but a tiny, blissed out smile curls her lips as I paint her cheeks with my release. My grip softens in her hair, and I cradle the side of her head as she sways on her knees.

She breathes hard for a minute. Gathers herself as my thumb rubs at her scalp, massaging her the way I did in the shower.

Then Natalia stares at the camera. She uses her pinkie fingertip to gather a bead of my come from her chin. And she sucks her finger clean.

"I'm sorry, Daddy," she rasps, shrugging like she's not sorry at all. "But I'm not coming home."

* * *

No man could deserve Natalia Volkova, but I deserve her even less than most. I kiss her forehead and help her to stand, spinning her around and bundling her into the bed. She smiles at me sleepily as I fuss over her, checking that she's comfortable and that she has enough pillows.

"Carver," she murmurs, amusement rich in her voice. "Stop fretting and come to bed."

It's so *domestic,* and I force myself not to fixate on what she told her father on camera. *I'm not coming home.* She can't have meant that she'd stay here—she must be leveraging this too, using it to improve her own life like the strategist she is.

Natalia is cunning. Resourceful. Perfection itself. I can't read too much into this. And I definitely have no right to the pinch of hurt in my chest.

It's not as though she owes me anything. What we have is not some sacred love story—I am her kidnapper. She can use me in turn however she likes.

"Carver?" She's slurring from tiredness, her face squashed against my pillow, and a wave of longing hits me so hard that I sway on the spot. It steals my breath, makes my ears ring, and *fuck*, if only I hadn't stolen her from her tent. If only I'd introduced myself in the daylight, spoken to her like a normal man—maybe I could have forgotten my mission against her family.

Maybe.

But then I'd never have felt her thrashing and fighting in my arms. I'd never have lashed her to my bed rail and seen her eyes light up with excitement. I'd never have seen that traitorous damp spot on the seam of her leggings, betraying the wicked fact that she liked it all too.

I cross to the desk, camera in hand, and begin the process of uploading the footage. If I were a good man, I'd delete it. Or at least I'd never send it. I'd erase this whole twisted game and let her go this instant, walking her back to her tent and setting her loose into the mountains.

I'm not a good man. I want her father to see the footage. Just the thought makes my skin heat with savage pleasure.

And though I'm not holding Natalia hostage anymore, I can't deliver her back to the real world.

Not tonight, anyway. The pale tinge of dawn is creeping through the trees outside the window, and Natalia is ashen with exhaustion. She's curled up in my bed like she belongs, her soft breaths drifting through the cabin.

Tomorrow. I set my jaw and vow to myself—tomorrow I will let her go.

I love Natalia Volkova. More than life. More than these mountains. More, even, than the sweet taste of revenge.

And because I love her, I will set her free.

Natalia

I wake to a sunlit cabin and the smell of pancakes and bacon. Stretching my arms overhead, I sigh happily and roll over, smoothing my hand across the mattress beside me.

The sheet is cold. Ice cold.

Carver didn't sleep here last night.

I frown and sit up, blinking the sleep from my eyes. He's here, by the kitchen range, dressed in worn jeans that cling to his long legs and a sage green flannel shirt. Carver's back is turned, his head bowed over the cooking breakfast, and unease prickles at the back of my neck.

"Carver?" He turns and throws me a smile over his shoulder, but it's all wrong. Polite. *Distant.*

"Breakfast is nearly ready. Do you want syrup on your pancakes?"

I nod, willing him to call me *princess.* He turns back to the range without another word, flipping a pancake with a spatula.

A cold, clammy sensation trickles down my spine. All the warmth of the morning slides away—the sunshine spilling golden through the windows, the leftover warmth from the fire, it's all chased away by shadows. I bite down hard on my tongue.

"What's going on?"

With my father, I always danced around my questions. Played it safe, lest he blow up in my face.

I'm done playing it safe. I'm no coward—not anymore.

Carver's shoulders tense, but his voice is steady. "I'm making breakfast. Brewing us coffee. Then you can have another shower if you like, and I'll walk you back to your tent."

My heart thuds in my chest. It beats slow and hard, my pulse roaring in my ears, and for a second I forget to breathe. My hands fist in the bed sheets, knuckles turning white, and I will myself to *stop feeling.*

When I suck in a ragged breath, Carver finally turns around. He's frowning, concerned, but what the hell does *that* matter? It's the polite concern of a host, not a lover. A host who's ready for me to leave.

"Natalia?"

I scramble out of bed, my legs wobbly as I stumble over the floorboards. I glance around, looking for my possessions before I remember that I was stolen here without warning. Holding my chin high, I march and scoop up my sleeping bag with all the dignity I can muster.

"Natalia," Carver barks. "You need to eat first."

I whirl on him, not bothering to hide the hurt etching my face. It's cracking me open, slicing up my insides, and I couldn't smooth it away if I tried.

Carver freezes, eyes wide.

"I don't want your *food.* You got what you wanted, is that it? You got your revenge, you had your fun, and now you're done. Time to ruin someone else's life." My laugh is hollow, so bitter, and Carver winces before he steps forward. He's still clutching a spatula in one hand, and for some reason that makes me want to scream.

"Goodbye, Carver," I spit, bundling the sleeping bag higher in my arms. "Do me a favor, okay? Go and jump off a cliff."

It's a lame parting line, but I don't even get to finish storming out. I yank his door open and march out onto the deck, but I don't even reach the first step before two arms cage me back against a hard chest. Carver lifts me easily, kicking and cursing in his hold, and carries me back into his cabin as I fight like a wildcat.

"Let me *go*," I yell as he drops me on his mattress. He reaches for the rope still tied around the bed rail, his expression calm. "You can't tell me to go and then tie you to your freaking bed!"

"No?" His fingers are quick, tying the knot around my wrists as I kick and fight, my puny noodle arms next to useless compared to his strength. "Looks like I just did, princess."

I yank on the ties, hard enough to rub my skin raw, and a scowl lowers over his features.

"Be careful," he says, voice dark. "I won't be happy if you hurt yourself."

"You *jerk*." I slump back against the mattress, suddenly exhausted. Tears well in my eyes, spilling down my cheeks, and how am I here again? In the one position that I woke up craving, and that now feels like a cruel joke.

He doesn't want me to stay. But he won't let me leave.

"Please." I screw my eyes shut. "Let me *go*."

The hurt that bloomed in my chest when he told me I'd be leaving today—it's spreading like a bruise through my body. My breaths are coming fast and ragged, and when fingertips trace my cheek, I tear my face away and bury it in the pillow.

"Princess."

"Go away." My yell is muffled by the fabric. The mattress dips as he sits beside me on the bed.

"Princess. Look at me."

"No."

"Natalia. *Please.*"

It's the desperate edge to his voice that makes me look over. Out of bitter curiosity more than anything else, but then I find his face open and raw. Carver gazes down at me with so much naked emotion that my chest throbs. I tug on my ties, lips parting as he watches me.

"I didn't realize." He frowns. "I'm your kidnapper, Natalia. I never dreamed that you would want to stay."

I blink at him. I can't move. Can't breathe. Can only lie perfectly still and strain to hear his quiet words.

"I've done so many bad things to you already." He traces my bottom lip with his thumb. "And princess, it's just the beginning. Stealing you away, tying you up—it's just the *start* of the bad things I want to do to you. Do you understand?"

I nod. Dazed. Not quite daring to hope.

I want him to do those things to me too.

Carver shakes my shoulder. Not hard enough to hurt, just to jar me back to the conversation.

"You're not gagged, Natalia. Tell me what you're thinking."

I lick my lips. And tell Carver the words that I can only admit to him. To the man who knows me, body and soul.

"I'm thinking... that I wish I *were* gagged."

Fierce hunger ripples through him. His eyes darken, his lip curls with savage satisfaction. A tendon stands out in his neck.

"Princess," Carver says, rough and tender. Then he snatches

up last night's gag and shoves it between my teeth.

He's not gentle with me. Not in these moments, and I relish every bruising grip, every yank at my clothes. Carver tears the shirt and sweatpants off me, splitting the fabric straight down the middle. And when he climbs onto the bed, kneeling between my trembling thighs, he grins as I kick at his chest.

"Easy, now." He catches my ankle and squeezes. "You'll only make this worse for yourself."

I growl and shake my head, thrashing and gnawing at the gag, and Carver laughs darkly as he runs one finger up my bared pussy. I'm drenched, dripping onto his bed sheets, and the sound of that smoky chuckle makes my hips twitch after his touch.

He tugs his shirt over his head. Unbuttons his jeans. And pulls out his cock.

"Mmph."

I yell into the gag, twisting and panting as Carver looms over me. He's big and bulky, the weight of him dipping the mattress, and his dark chest hair tickles over my skin. He pauses at my entrance, jaw clenched tight, and forces me to look at him.

"Are you sure?" he asks, hunger still burning in his eyes, but there's more there, too. Care. *Love.*

I nod quickly. I want this more than anything, more than can be healthy, and I bracket his hips with my thighs and squeeze. His mouth quirks and then his broad head nudges me, pushing inside my entrance. It's a stretching, burning sensation and I let out a whimper as the first inch disappears inside me.

A cool palm smooths over my forehead, brushing away the hair.

"It'll be okay. Just a bit of pain at the start, and then I'll make you feel so good, princess."

I nod weakly, breath hitching as he slides in another inch. I'm so wet that there's barely any resistance—only the tightness of my muscles. I force myself to relax, dragging in a low breath and imagining myself melting into the mattress. It helps, another few inches sliding inside me, and Carver murmurs soft praise into my hair.

"Fuck. You feel so good. So perfect, Natalia. This pussy was made for me. Made for me to tie up and fuck. I'll never let you leave. Never let you out of my goddamn sight."

I nod, heat prickling over my skin at his words. The stretch of him still stings, but there's something else there now too. A delicious tickling sensation, a perfect kind of friction, and I lift my hips to chase it. Carver chokes out a low laugh and seals his mouth to mine, pressing the rest of his cock inside me.

It's *big.* I'm so stretched and full and my heart is brimming over in tandem. Especially when Carver grits out a dark curse and begins to move, hips pumping, gentle at first until that rough edge I love comes back. His hips slam into mine and I lift up to meet him, tugging on the rope tying my wrist and savoring the scrape on my skin.

With anyone else, I'd feel deviant. Sick. But with Carver… I'm home.

He matches my darkness, meets it with his own, and I decide here and now that it doesn't matter if he tries to do the right thing. If he tries to take me back to my tent.

He brought me here. Showed me how love can feel. Let me into his home and his heart, taught me the sweetness of pain, and ensnared himself too in the process.

I'll never leave. Whatever he tries.

He's not the only one with no limits.

"Stay with me," he grinds out, like he can hear what I'm thinking. "Stay here in my cabin. Don't go. Don't ever fucking go." His face is pressed against my collarbone, licking and biting, and when I nod my chin scrapes his hair. Carver groans, digging his fingers into my hips, and slams into me over and over. It's too much and it's perfect, a sweet overload of sensation, and my toes curl against the backs of his legs as he rubs against my clit.

"There's only you, Natalia. Only you in the whole goddamn world. Just your sweet face and your wicked smile and your clever mind. And this *pussy*."

His fingers dig deep into my hips, deep enough to bruise, his thrusts becoming crazed. I arch my back, seeking the friction I need, and he rubs over my clit in a way that makes my body *sing*.

My orgasm is like the storms that haunt the mountains. It rolls in slowly at first, but as it fills me, it crackles with power. I bite down hard on the gag, wrists tugging on the rope, and lock my thighs tight around Carver's hips. And I *come*.

He pushes up on his hands, staring at me as wave after wave of sensation rolls through me, tightening around his cock. Sweat beads of my forehead and my cheeks flush, and still he watches me like I'm the answer to all his prayers.

"Fuck," he mutters as I finally slump back against the mattress. Carver licks a stripe up my throat and slams into me once, twice, three more times.

Warmth spreads through my pussy. Carver hovers over me, muscles shaking, as he gives me everything. Every last drop.

I hitch my legs tighter, drawing him deeper into me.

I'm not going anywhere. And neither is he.

Carver

Three Years Later

I prowl silently through the forest, pine needles carpeting my steps. The crisp air of fall swirls around my cheeks, and birds call out overhead in the trees, but I ignore it all. My eyes are fixed on one thing.

My wife.

She's up ahead at the stream, our baby girl balanced on her hip. She stands at the edge of the water, pointing at something and talking to our daughter. Ava kicks her legs and waves a pudgy arm, her cheeks ruddy with excitement, and I hide a smile as I step closer. A twig snaps under my boot and I duck behind a tree, heart slamming in my chest.

It's a game we play. My wife likes to be followed. And I like to stalk her through the mountains.

"Oh!" She splays a hand on her chest and laughs when I finally step out of the trees, just a few feet down the bank. "You got me that time."

Ava spots me and cries out too, a happy, gurgling noise.

Has any man ever been this lucky? I come to stand with my chest to Natalia's back, smoothing a hand over her rounded belly. Over our next son or daughter, just waiting to join us.

"Did it work?" Natalia's words sound light, but I can hear the nerves burning beneath them. When I told her my plan a few months ago to get my father's shares in the Volkov empire back, I'd worried that she would balk. That her loyalty to her father would finally win out. But my princess smirked and nodded, pulling my notes closer so she could add her thoughts.

"You're sure?" I'd asked her. Her family may have cut her off when she stayed with me, but they're still her blood. I'd never do anything that might hurt her.

"I'm sure." Natalia had cuddled Ava close, bending to sniff the crown of her downy head. "The Volkovs have enough money." She smirked, wicked and bright. "I want Ava to have a slice."

Stress had dogged my every waking moment since that conversation, but this morning, several million dollars landed in our bank account. I came here to tell her. To see the relief in her eyes.

Natalia doesn't disappoint.

"Carver!" She throws her free arm around my neck, squeezing tight. "Oh my god. I can't believe it."

I can. Anything is possible with Natalia by my side.

"What do you think, baby girl?" She jiggles Ava on her hip. "Will you want to go to college?" Ava giggles, her little chin wet with drool, and I throw my head back and laugh. A bird bursts out of a nearby tree, the stream rushes past over the rocks, and everything is perfect. Perfect.

"Don't pressure her," I warn, and Natalia gives me a scathing look. Just like I knew she would. After growing up under her parents' tight control, Natalia is determined to let our daughter choose her own path.

"Of course not." Natalia blows a raspberry on Ava's cheek. "Us Ennox women know our own minds."

Ennox. Hearing her call herself that, hearing Natalia take my name... Joy and pride and hunger surge in me, and I press a searing kiss to her neck.

She's mine. *Mine.* Forever.

I'm hers.

And we're never letting go.

II

Desert Target

Description

They hired me to kill the queen of the underworld. But when I track my target into the desert, she's... a hairdresser?

I need to get out of this life. But first, I need money, so I take one last job—a hit on the notorious Viper.

The Viper is evil. Unhinged. She's killed hundreds of innocents. But when I track her to the desert, she's... on vacation?

This isn't the Viper. It's some poor gorgeous doppelganger who floors me with a single blink of her doe eyes.

But I'm not the only one with a case of mistaken identity. And the desert is a dangerous place.

I hope the hairdresser likes big, brutal hitmen. Because I'm her ticket to survive.

Leif

I duck inside the shadowy bar, keeping my disgust at the stale beer smell off my face. It's not 10am yet, and there are women dressed in sequined bikinis spinning lazily around poles. Men crowd around the stages—not as many as in the nights, no doubt, but still enough to be really damn depressing. They're deep in their drinks, slurring encouragement at the girls as they dance with bored expressions on their faces.

Jesus. This bar is the end of the earth.

I stride past the stages without a second glance. No offense to the women—they're just making a living, same as anyone else, and god knows *I* can't judge—but I'm here for a reason. A meeting with a contact.

And besides, these dancers aren't my type. Sure, I don't know *what* my type is, only that I haven't found it yet.

The room stinks of cigarette smoke, spilled drinks, and overzealous body spray. The light from the street barely makes it through the grubby windows, and I have to squint through the gloom as I walk past the booths. The hackles rise on the back of my neck—I don't like being vulnerable, and this shadowy bar with its pounding music and drunken crowds is a criminal's perfect hunting ground.

It would be *my* perfect hunting ground, if I ever had a mark as stupid as those baying men.

"What is this dive?" I grumble when I find my contact sitting at a table in the corner. It's the darkest part of the bar, far from the stages and any nosy bartenders, and I'm relieved to see the drink in front of Z is orange juice. "There had better not be vodka in that," I add, sliding into the chair opposite him.

Z. That's all I know about the man I've worked with for the last six years. Ever since I got into this line of work, Z has been my contact. My *handler*. And all I know about him is his first initial.

"How's it going, Zack? Zayne? Zander?" This is part of our routine. I hazard a few guesses and he rolls his eyes, shaking his grizzled head. Z can't be more than mid-thirties, but with his sallow skin and thinning hair, he looks decades older.

That's what this life will do to you, if you let it. That's why I'm getting out, before it's too late for me too. I'm going to take one last job, top up the savings I've been building, and start a new life. A better one. One where I try and figure out what, exactly, my type might be.

"You're going to Morocco." Z cuts straight to the point, his chair creaking as he leans forward. A plain folder lands on the table in front of me, and I peel it off the sticky wood with a grimace. "Fair warning: it's a woman."

I toss the folder back down without bothering to open it.

"No. You know I don't kill innocents."

Z snorts. "Who said anything about innocent? Women can be pieces of shit, too, L. Get with the times." He leans back and clasps his hands over his gut, smirking like he just won a huge argument. Whatever. I roll my eyes but flip the folder open. I can't claim that I'm not intrigued.

The glossy photos slither out from under their paperclip. The target is young, early twenties maybe, with shoulder-length blonde hair and hard blue eyes. In the first photo, she's climbing out of an armored car somewhere in Eastern Europe. She stares around the street, grim satisfaction on her face, and something about those dead eyes makes me shiver.

Yeah. Okay, I see it now. Something's not right with this chick.

I flip to the next photo. It's grainy, like a screenshot of web footage. She's got a scarf wrapped over her face as she stands in the mountains, her arms crossed and a truck full of weapons behind her.

The third photo is the one that makes me pause. It's the same woman, the same shoulder-length blonde hair and piercing blue eyes, but the photographer must have caught her off guard. She seems softer in this one. She's smiling gently at her phone, standing alone on a city street, and instead of all blacks and grays, she's wearing a white cotton t-shirt, jeans, and pink sneakers.

"It's the Viper," Z says quickly, like he can sense my resolve fading. "You've heard of her, right? The arms dealer and drug runner? She's killed hundreds, L. Ruined thousands of lives."

I blow out a hard breath, eyes still fixed on the photo. *This* woman is the Viper? Well, shit. I think I just found my type. I've sure as hell never reacted to a woman like this before—with a knot twisting in my chest, so tight my breaths come quick. My blood thrums under my skin, heating me up, and my throat is suddenly dry.

I should have bought a drink after all.

"You're sure?" My voice sounds like gravel. "You're sure she really did all that?"

Z scoffs. "Yeah. I'm sure. We didn't mix up the queen of the underworld with someone else."

Damn. Something about this doesn't sit right with me, but then neither do weapons dealing and drug running. I may be a hardened bastard, one with more blood on my hands than I'll ever wash off, but at least I have a code. A way of trying to live right, at least as well as I can.

And after one more hit, I'll be free. I'll have enough saved to start over, to start fresh, and the images I've been dreaming of for years float before my eyes.

My own ranch, with stables of horses.

A quiet cabin in the mountains.

Or a boat. Something sturdy enough to sail around the world.

There are so many options. So many ways my life could go. And after thirty-four years of shitty luck and hard knocks, I'm ready for some good surprises. All I need is one more hit—to take this (okay yes, female) monster out and make the world a slightly better place.

"I'll do it," I grunt before I can change my mind, swiping the folder off the table. It crackles as it peels off the sticky wood, and I level Z a look. "Next time, set up the meet in a coffee shop or some shit. Come on, man."

"Next time?" Z asks mildly, and I catch myself. That's right. There will be no next time.

"Forget it." I grin, savage, and pleasure curls through me as the other man cringes back in his chair. "Slip of the tongue."

I don't say goodbye as I push to my feet and stride back

across the bar. That's not how this works. We're not friends, I don't even know his goddamn name, and we owe each other exactly nothing. That's how all my relationships have been.

Yeah. I'm ready for a change.

An image floats across my mind unbidden. A soft mouth curling up in a smile; a tumble of golden blonde hair.

No. I shove that thought away. It doesn't matter how cute her pink sneakers are. Doesn't matter that she looks good enough to eat. The woman in that photo is a cancer on the world—she ruins lives and gets rich doing it.

Me, I end lives. No two ways about it. I'm the best hit man on this continent.

But as least I live by a code. The Viper can't say that.

Hannah

The heat hits me the second I step off the plane, beaming as I make my way down the rickety metal stairs. The sky is big and blue, yawning wide open overhead, and the bright sunshine glints off the vehicles scattered over the tarmac. There's the baggage truck, our suitcases being tossed in a pile roughly enough that I cringe.

My poor straighteners. They were brand new last month.

Besides the baggage truck, with its loud men in fluorescent jackets, a passenger bus idles beside the plane, its doors propped open. We file on one by one, squashing in like sardines, and I make sure I'm pressed right up by the window.

I don't want to miss a second of this. Not one drop of buttery sunshine.

It's been cloudy and dull for *months* on the east coast, and in the end, that's what made me do it. What made me pick out a package tour, holding my breath as I squealed and pressed 'Confirm'. I've talked about this for so long, saving up and dreaming, and I can't believe it's finally happened.

I'm across the ocean in Morocco. In a brand new country, with a different culture, a different language. I'm here all on my own—with the tour, anyway—and I paid for every cent. Pride swells me so big, I'm surprised I don't drift up like a balloon and bob against the bus ceiling. I did it! I did it. Oh my gosh.

The doors slide closed with a hiss and the bus rocks into motion. It's a short drive along the tarmac to the airport doors, to passport control and baggage collection and the lobby where I'm meeting the tour group. I grip the nearest metal bar tightly, nerves fluttering in my stomach, but a few long breaths help me to calm back down.

Of course everyone won't hate me. I'm nice! And I've had a ton of practice talking to strangers as a hairdresser. And even if they *did* all hate me for some weird reason, I'm still here. Doing this big, scary thing. Taking one of my long-held dreams and making it happen. I dig out my phone from my back pocket and pull up Grandma's text for the millionth time.

Grandma: So proud of you, Hannah-Banana! Ride on a camel for me. xxx

I will. Grandma is a big part of the reason I picked Morocco. When I was growing up and my poor Mom was working two jobs to make ends meet, I spent so many afternoons and weekends at Grandma's, watching old movies. We liked the grainy adventure movies best, *especially* ones in the desert.

The Sahara. That's where I'm going. To see those red sand dunes with my own two eyes, and to make my Grandma proud.

* * *

My cheeks are flushed and sweaty by the time I lug my wheeled

71

suitcase into the airport lobby. The little wheel on the left keeps catching, spinning out like a wild supermarket cart, and I'm beginning to think bringing a hot pink suitcase wasn't the best idea. People keep staring, especially men, their eyes lingering on my bare shoulders beneath my yellow tank top.

"Sorry!" My suitcase bounces off a trash can, the sound echoing through the lobby. A man in a fluorescent vest with a radio glares. "Sorry. I'm not great at this bit."

He shakes his head, bored, and turns back to his crackling radio, muttering something under his breath. I smile harder, trying to ignore the sinking feeling in my stomach as I battle my way across the lobby. I force myself to look at the huge glass windows instead, to focus on the huge shafts of sunshine spilling through the clean glass.

It's beautiful. And the bustle is wonderful—a tangle of manic energy that buoys me back to a good mood. By the time I find my tour group, the leader holding a battered cardboard sign with all our names on, I'm back on cloud nine.

"Hi!" I drag my suitcase into the circle and dump it with the other luggage before brushing off my hands. "I'm Hannah. I'm a hairdresser. I'm so excited to be here."

I'm blathering—come on, no one cares about my job!—but everyone nods and says hi, and I blow out a relieved sigh. An older woman standing next to me pats my arm, and her kind, crinkly eyes remind me of Grandma.

"Nice to meet you, dear." Her Scottish burr is hard to understand, but I get the gist of it. I beam at her, then peer around the rest of the group. We're a ragtag bunch, a weird selection of all ages, thrown together for one purpose: to experience the wonders of the desert.

I can't wait. Oh my gosh, I can't wait. I bounce on my heels as the last few stragglers arrive, their faces drawn from the long plane ride. No one else has a hot pink suitcase, but the Scottish woman—Maggie—has a old-fashioned holdall with a stag pattern, and someone else has a collection of superhero badges sewn onto their case.

"Alright." Our guide tosses his cardboard sign onto a nearby seat and claps his hands together. "Welcome to Morocco. Does everyone have everything they need?"

I think of my new straighteners. My digital camera, my back-up disposable camera, and the brand new first aid kit in the bottom of my suitcase. Our tour may only be a week long, but I packed a month's worth of clothes, just in case.

Oh, I'm ready.

Sahara, here I come.

Leif

I have a ritual when I take on a job.

I do my research. Read the folder a dozen times, absorbing every detail about the life I'm going to end. The person's weaknesses and strengths. The risks of the operation. Most importantly: why they deserve the hit.

I'm no hero. But a man needs a code.

Reading up on the Viper turns my stomach. She may look like an angel in the photo I saved, smiling softly down at her phone. But the trail of destruction behind this woman is inevitable. She's gotta go.

After I've read the file, I move on to my own research. Learning the mark's habits; feeling out the best method for the job. The reason I'm the best hitman, the most *expensive* hired killer on the continent, is because I'm quiet. Clean. I don't leave any mess behind me. No scandals. No repercussions.

You've got to get close for that. Close enough to be alone with the mark, for a few seconds at least. That's tricky in the desert. That's how I find myself in a loose cotton shirt, worn canvas pants and leather boots, a chunky camera slung around my neck. Just another tourist in the wild, romantic landscape. Nothing to see here.

"Busy?" I ask a man with a stall by the side of the road. We're in a small town, a tiny cluster of buildings before the roads give way to rolling red sands in the distance. The Viper passed this way with her group two hours ago. I know, because I was watching, a pair of binoculars pressed to my eyes.

I can't make sense of the group she's with. The queen of the underworld must travel with lackeys, sure—but burly meatheads with wires and guns, not doddering old ladies and pairs of laughing teenagers.

It must be deep cover. She must be planning something *big*. It's the only way this makes sense.

"Earlier, yes. Now? No. No buyers." The man nods pointedly at the jars of fresh honey lining his rickety stall. I dig in my pocket, pulling out a few coins while my mind drifts. She passed through here. Is she headed into the Sahara?

What is it—a weapons drop? A meeting with other kingpins? What the hell is she doing out here?

I drop the money on the table and swipe up a random jar. Better to blend in than raise questions.

I catch up with the group just before midday, when their guides set up tents for shade and serve mint tea and sliced oranges. I watch them through a rifle scope, lying flat out on the burning sand, as the Viper throws back her blonde head and laughs at something the old woman said.

A cruel joke, probably. Some twisted humor.

It doesn't matter. Her time is almost up.

I adjust the scope, bringing her in to sharper focus, and a drumbeat starts in my chest. Her blonde hair brushes over her collarbone, an oversized pair of sunglasses perched on her pert little nose, and a sliver of her white bra strap peeks out from her tank top. I watch, mouth drier than the dune I'm lying on, as she squeezes a dollop of sun cream into her palm and spreads it over her bare shoulders.

She doesn't *look* like an international criminal. Hell, she hasn't stopped smiling for a single moment that I've been watching her. My finger twitches against the trigger, but this isn't my method anyway. I need to get close to her.

God, do I need to get closer.

The Viper lifts an orange wedge to her lips and bites down, a trickle of juice running down her chin.

Jesus Christ. I want to lick her clean. I want to tip her head back and devour her fruity mouth.

It's the sun. The heat. The dehydration. There's no other reason I'd be panting after a mark. Not after I read the worst things she's ever done. Not after I read the headlines; saw the body counts; saw the photos of unhinged destruction. Lots of people hallucinate in the desert; a stray thought about a beautiful woman means nothing.

And god, she is beautiful, no matter how terrible. Grown men would fight for the chance to kiss her sandal-clad feet. *I'd* walk barefoot through the scorpions just to smell her neck.

Good thing I need to get closer anyway. Close enough to kill her. I pack up my rifle, expertly keeping the grains of sand away, and stow the case in my black backpack. The guides with her group are packing up the tents, and the strange assortment of men and women are piling into their off-roaders.

I wait until the kicked-up sand of their trail settles again before following on my rented dirt bike. And something loosens in my chest as I push off, chasing after her.

Leif

I don't want the Viper out of my sight.

* * *

Night falls with a vengeance in the desert. It's a deeper, inkier darkness than I've ever seen, with galaxies of stars winking overhead. The heat from the sun leeches away, down into the sand, and a chill whistles through the dunes.

A campfire flickers in the valley between two sand dunes, three large tents clustered around. The Viper is cunning to come out here to conduct her business. There are no straining ears, no prying eyes. Well, none except mine. And I watch her without blinking as she settles onto a camp chair, a bowl of something steaming cradled in her lap. She eats delicately, eyes closing in bliss at the first mouthful, and for a moment I forget why I'm watching her.

I'd follow this woman for the sake of it. For the pleasure of watching her go through her day. When she tipped back her head and swigged from a water bottle earlier, her pale throat bobbing, I had to stifle a groan.

I'll kill her quickly. I have to—every minute I spend following her, my resolution fades a bit more.

The group stays around the fire until the flames die down and only glowing embers remain. Then they excuse themselves one by one, ducking through the tent doorways with only the stars to light their way. There's one tent for women, one for men, and one for the guides. A strange arrangement for a crime boss. But then, the Viper is nothing like I expected. Maybe this too is to throw her rivals off.

The sand shifts under my boots as I creep over the dunes, staying far from the dying glow of the fire. Low voices murmur to each other, punctuated by soft peals of laughter, as the group readies themselves for bed.

No watch? No one left on guard? The Viper is truly too comfortable in these dunes. I steal through the sands like a shadow, rounding the back of the women's tent and finding a slit in the canvas. My knife slides silently out of my belt, the steel glinting in the silvery starlight. I grip it tight, straining to hear the Viper, when a body bursts out of the gap in the tent.

"Oh! Haha. Sorry, I need to pee." The Viper brushes past me, patting my chest as she goes. I blink after her, clenching the knife handle tighter.

It's perfect. We're out here alone, away from everyone else, and her guard is down. I won't get this chance again.

She doesn't notice me following her until she's well over the dune, dipping below the crest. She turns and begins to hitch up her long skirt before she sees me, dropping the fabric with a gasp.

"Oh! Sorry. I thought I'd gone far enough. Are you..." She falters as I keep approaching. "Are you with the guides? I don't—I don't recognize you—"

I clap my hand over her mouth, muffling her squeak of alarm.

"Drop the act, Viper. We both know why I'm here."

Hannah

Um. Are there some desert adventure extras on this tour that I didn't read about? I didn't see anything about role play, but then Grandma's always telling me off for skimming and not paying attention.

Whoever this guy is, he's a great actor. And the knife in his hand looks super authentic. I'd be scared out my mind, but he called me *Viper*, and there's no way *that's* real. It's just like the old movies I used to watch with Grandma. A mysterious stranger appears in the desert, with a story for the campfire and a treasure map or something.

I tug at his shirt, and after a second, he moves his hand away from my mouth just by an inch.

"Can we do this in a second?" I whisper. "Sorry. I don't mean to throw you off. But I drank three big cups of mint tea and I'm about to burst."

"I—what?" Even in the darkness, I can see him frown. His craggy eyebrows lower, his smooth forehead creasing, and there's something so *stern* about him that I shiver. I suddenly

79

notice how tall this stranger is. How broad his shoulders are. How good he smells—like soap and sandalwood.

"The role play. Or the activity, or whatever. Can I pee first?"

"The role play," he says flatly.

"Yeah. But don't be put off! I'm super excited. I love stuff like this. Last summer I went to a renaissance fair, and I dressed in a princess gown and dropped a hanky at the jousting and everything." He blinks at me, silent, and I take that as a yes. "Be right back." I pat his arm, and *damn,* that's a bicep. "Um. Don't listen, okay?"

He grumbles something but nods, and I jog away over the sand, far enough that he won't be able to see me. I gather up my skirt, hoping and praying that there are no scorpions down there in the shadows, and squat down to do my business.

"I'm back!" I stage whisper as I jog back across the dunes. He jerks around, apparently lost in some daze. "I've forgotten the opening bit though. Do you mind starting over?" He stares at me blankly as I come to a stop in front of him.

Poor guy. I've thrown him completely off his rhythm. I get like this sometimes too, when I'm in the zone in the salon and then someone interrupts me to ask a question. It takes me a few seconds to remember where I was and what I was doing. I take him by the wrist, determined to be helpful.

"Here." I clap his hand back over my mouth. His palm is warm and dry, with calluses on the skin. I nod up at him, encouraging.

"I don't..." He frowns down at me, eyes hard. They're pale gray in the moonlight, deepening to charcoal when his face is in shadow. "Who are you? What is this?"

Oh dear. I've really ruined this for him. I peel his hand off my mouth again, my hand wrapped around his wrist. He's so big, so muscly and strong, that my thumb and fingers don't meet. Dark hairs dust his corded forearms, and a sleek watch brings out his tan. He's so *masculine*.

"Don't be shy. No one heard our false start. And if the tour company gives you trouble, I'll just tell them it's my fault. I wish I'd never thrown you off, but I *really* had to pee." I nod at the knife clutched loosely in his hand. "You held that to my throat. Gosh, it looks so real, doesn't it? When I did community theater, you could tell the knives were fake from the back row. They looked like foil wrapped around cardboard. Well, I guess they *were* foil wrapped around cardboard..."

I trail off. I always talk too much when I'm nervous.

"I've ruined this, haven't I? Do you want to do your bit with one of the other tourists instead?" My shoulders slump, but I force my voice to stay bright. No point being a baby about it. "That's fine. Shall I fetch Maggie? She'll laugh so hard when you grab her—"

"Please." He tugs his hand away. "Stop talking."

"Oh." My heart sinks.

We stand there for a long moment, the silence thrumming between us. By the feel of it, my cheeks are on *fire*. He opens his mouth like he's going to say something else, but I step back.

"Okay. Um. I'll leave it with you, then."

Why? This is such a *me* thing to do. I save up for ages, fly halfway around the world, all for these experiences, and then I can't shut up long enough to enjoy them. I don't know who I was kidding, coming all this way on my own. I walk back toward the tent with stiff arms.

"Wait." A hand grips my shoulder. It's not gentle, it's kind of rough actually, and I should probably hate that. Should knock him away and be offended. But I must have a one way ticket to hell, because my knees go all gooey under his grip. A shiver runs through my body, heat flushes over my skin, and I suck in a shaky breath.

Who *is* this man?

"Yes?" I spin back to him, hopeful. Hopeful for *what*, I don't know; I can't even name these feelings coursing through me. I only know that whatever he has planned, I want him to do it to me and no one else. Even if it's scripted, even if it's part of the game for him to touch me, I want it. I want it so bad. I've only spent a few minutes with him, but already his quiet, steady presence has sucked me in. Every glance from him, every muttered sentence—I crave it.

"Viper." That's all he says. Just that word, then he peers at me, waiting for some reaction.

"Um. Is that a cue? Am I supposed to say something? I'm sorry, I didn't see anything about this in the brochure—"

He reels back, tearing his hand away from my shoulder. I miss that warm weight as soon as it's gone. It anchored me down to the sand, made me feel rooted and safe. With it gone, I might spiral off in the breeze.

"What is your name?" he asks, voice rough. "Who are you?"

I frown. Is this part of it? Maybe one of the others paid extra for this, and I'm accidentally stealing their activity.

"I'm Hannah." I wait, but he says nothing. Shows no sign of recognition. "You know. The American? The hairdresser? Were we supposed to sign up for this separately? Because it depends how much it costs, obviously, but if I can afford it I'd definitely like to do this activity—"

Two firm hands land on my shoulders. They squeeze and mold me, and I sigh, my head tipping back.

"Hannah."

"Uh-huh?" My eyelids flutter closed. His thumbs rub circles on the base of my neck, right where my muscles are stiff from the flight, and I stifle a groan, swaying under his touch. He's a wizard. He's put me in a trance with a single squeeze.

"Hannah the hairdresser," he repeats.

My mouth quirks up. "That's me." This guy's kind of funny. It's like it's his first day on the job. "So what happens next? Are there other actors here?"

"No," he murmurs. "I'm here to kill you."

Leif

She bursts out laughing. *Laughing.* Her eyes light up with excitement, and not it's not the predatory thrill of another criminal. It's the sweet, guileless excitement of a tourist on vacation.

Hannah. Hannah the *hairdresser.*

I'm going to fucking kill Z. So much for up-to-date information on the Viper.

Hannah tosses her head back as she laughs, her blonde hair silvery in the starlight, and I want to plunge my hands into those tresses. Feel the silky strands run between my fingers; grab a handful and tug as I fuck her from behind. She's smaller than me, petite and curvy, and all I can think about is the way my hands would fit on the swells of her body. How tiny and toy-like she'd be in my grip.

Shit. *Shit.* This woman cannot be my type. I can't—I can't go there. I'd ruin her.

"Hannah," I grit out, jerking her shoulder so she hushes down. "I'm being serious."

"Oh, right," she crows, reaching for my knife. "I suppose this is real—ow!" She snatches her hand back, staring wide-eyed at the red line on her fingertip. We both watch as a crimson bead of blood swells up from the cut, quivers, then drops into the sand.

She sucks in a breath. A fill-your-lungs-to-scream kind of breath. I clap my hand over her mouth for the third time tonight.

"Quiet," I tell her urgently, bundling her wriggling body up into my arms. She kicks and thrashes—she's a fighter, I realize with pride—but her soft, small body is no match against my burly frame. I carry her over the dunes, away from the tent and the dying campfire, and the only sound is her panicked, muffled cries against my palm. Her breath is hot and damp, and a row of sharp teeth sink into my skin, but I grit my jaw and ignore the hot pinch of pain.

She doesn't understand yet how much danger she's in.

But I do.

If Z mistook her for a sighting of the Viper, others will have too. And they'd be fools not to take this opportunity—to strike at the mobster queen while she's seemingly unprotected.

I should walk away. Dump Hannah on the sand and take off for the road—back to civilization and a chance for another job. She's not my problem, doppelganger or not. And a sweet, everyday girl like that...

No one would ever know what happened to her. Whatever family she left at home—whatever *boyfriend*, I think sourly—they'd never get the truth. That Hannah was killed for looking like another woman.

I know that I should walk away, but damn me, I can't. Some powerful urge keeps my arms banded tight around her, my hand clasped over her mouth. I could no more leave this woman in danger than I could jump off a plane without a parachute.

I push those unsettling thoughts away. It—it doesn't matter. I'll get her to safety, and that will be that. I'll disappear like smoke, going back underground, and then I'll examine these feelings at a safe distance.

Her heel glances off my shin, the force reverberating through the bone, and I curse under my breath. Already, she's caused me so much trouble. So when we reach my hidden dirt bike and I bundle her sideways across my lap, still kicking, I don't gentle my voice when I snap at her.

"Lie still, you little fool. I'm trying to save your life."

She pauses in her kicking for half a breath, blinking up at me. Her eyes are wide, her cheeks flushed bright red, and something twists in my chest. I brush a strand of hair off her forehead. She whimpers and cringes away.

That's it. I need to remember this moment; this honest reaction from her. I'm a scary motherfucker, the sort of man she should avoid, and we both know it. She doesn't feel this pull the same way I do.

I'll take her to Marrakesh. Leave her in the airport to survive as best she can. That's all I can offer; hell, it's more than she even wants from me. So I tell her, in quiet tones, that I'm taking her back to the city. That she's not safe here. That a hit has been taken out on her by mistake. And most of all, that she needs to get back on a plane and disappear back into her ordinary life.

"But…" Hannah sniffs, wriggling to sit up on the bike. She grabs my thigh as she swings a leg over, and at least she's not fighting. "I don't have my suitcase."

"Your suit—" I cut myself off, pinching the bridge of my nose. The kernel of a headache is forming behind my right eye. "It doesn't matter. Do you understand? You. Are. In. Danger."

She huffs, crossing her arms. "And do *you* understand that I need a passport to fly? Asshole."

Fuck. She's right. I'm so used to crossing borders and moving around the world unseen. I forget how regular people do it. But she will need her passport, won't she, and her money and whatever other crap she has in her baggage. I sigh and grab the backpack I stashed by my bike, tugging the zip down and pulling out the folder on the Viper.

"Read this." I don't want any more trouble. If she reads that folder and still wants to stay—well, that's natural selection. "I'll get your case."

"It's the bright pink one," she chirps up as I swing a leg back off the bike. Of course it is. I watch her closely, my muscles tensed and ready to pounce, but she doesn't try to hop back down off the seat. She flips the folder open and squints at the pages, trying to read in the dim starlight.

"Stay here," I grumble, but she doesn't nod. Doesn't acknowledge me at all. She holds the folder up, a few inches from her nose, frowning prettily at the pages, and *shit*, there's something wrong with my heart. I'm having some kind of episode out here in the desert.

I need to retire. That's it. I need to find this stupid pink suitcase, and I need to drop Hannah somewhere safe, and get out of this nonsense.

Forget the ranch. Forget the sailboat. I have enough money. This is it. I'm done.

Hannah

Okay, if this folder is a prop, it's a really freaking good one. Just like that knife. My tummy churns as I squint at the pages, the real details about my life, but jumbled up with this other woman's. The Viper. Just like the man called me outside the tent.

I don't think this is a vacation activity. I don't this is a joke at all. I whip my head around, pulse thrumming under my skin, but where can I go? I'm in the freaking Sahara. I'm at the mercy of the tour company that brought me here, and of this strange man who bundled me onto this bike.

The man who picked me up like I weighed nothing. Who carried me as easily as a kitten, firm but gentle in equal measures.

Oh, god. I fan my cheeks, trying desperately to *think*. But it's so hard, when I can still smell his manly scent. Can feel the tingle of his fingertips brushing over my forehead. Something clenches, deep inside my core, and I shift on the bike seat.

Come on. Come *on*. If it's real, if this is all happening…

and how would he have these details about me otherwise? My ticket details, my phone provider, even that photo of me back in Boston. How would he know all that if this was a prank? If he was insane?

He wouldn't. So this must be real. *Especially* since the woman in two of those photos is not me, but is like looking in a mirror.

The Viper. Gosh. What a horrible name. If I were a mobster, my code name would be way cuter.

"You're still here. Good." The man reemerges from the gloom, my suitcase tucked under his arm. He carries it like it weighs nothing, and I bite my lip. It's kind of hot. "What the hell have you got in here anyway, bricks? Bags of sand?"

Never mind.

"Just the essentials." I'm breathless as he lashes the case to the back of the bike. It rocks from the motion—the bike is pretty small to begin with, and with both of us and my suitcase, it looks like one of those tragically overloaded donkeys. The man sits behind me, his chest sealed to my back, so close that I can feel every ridge of muscle. Every thump of his heart. His big arms cage me in and he takes the handlebars, kicking the dirt bike to life.

The engine sputters loudly, the sound echoing through the desert. Over by the tents in the distance, shouts go up.

"Hold on, angel. We're getting out of here."

My tummy lurches, and we take off through the dunes.

* * *

I should be freaking out more. Did I hit my head? Maybe it's the glittering blanket of stars, and the shadowy landscape of dunes. None of this feels quite real. If anything, as the bike trundles beneath us, and I'm caged in tight by a pair of strong thighs and muscled arms, I feel... safe. Relaxed, even. Without thinking, I melt back against my... savior? Kidnapper? And he grunts and tucks my head under his chin.

He's warm, so warm and hard and safe, and my eyelids droop as we weave through the towering sand dunes. It's beautiful, a magical landscape, but it all looks so similar that I can't tell how much time is passing. We could be driving for minutes or hours or half the night, but I spend it leaning back against the man in a daze.

"What's your name?" I shout over the engine at one point. I can't keep calling him *the man* in my head. Not least because he's like no other man I've met. That word seems too weak for him. Like calling a tiger a kitty.

He says nothing for a long time, and I think he must not have heard. But then finally he speaks, the words rumbling through his chest against my shoulder blades.

"Leif. My name is Leif."

"Leaf?" I shake my head. There must be sand in my ears. But his chuckle is dark and gravelly. Like he doesn't laugh much.

"No. *Leif*. It's Norwegian. Leif Larsen."

Norwegian? I file that away, like a squirrel hiding sweet tidbits for later. I sigh and squirm back against him, trying to get comfy on this horrible bike, and he grunts again, a big palm landing on my thigh and forcing me to sit still.

"Enough."

What? I'm just trying to be comfortable. But when I ignore him, shuffling around again, I feel it. The rock-hard length jutting into my back.

I've never seen a man's... *thing*. Up close and in person.

And I've definitely never touched one. But it's touching *me*, digging into me through our layers of clothes, and somehow that makes me flush hot all over. I'm squirming again but for a different reason, because I'm restless and fidgety, and no matter how I sit on this vibrating bike, I can't *calm down*. Leif hears my whimpers, and his thumb strokes over my thigh.

"Nearly there," he rumbles in my ear. "There's an abandoned camp we'll stay in for the night. Then we'll leave again at dawn."

Dawn. Oh dear. *I'm on vacation*, I want to yell. Vacation and dawn should not go together! But then I remember the folder in his backpack, and the cut on my fingertip from his knife, and the ridiculous situation I'm in comes crashing back down. And I know I should be more scared, but it's hard to be frightened when I'm cradled between Leif's hard thighs. So the main question running through my head is: how am I ever going to afford another vacation? Will this happen every time I try to go away? My chin wobbles, and I press back against his chest.

It's just not *fair*.

I barely notice the camp before it lurches up out of the sand. When Leif said *camp*, I figured he meant an abandoned ratty tent, but this an old stone tower. Like an ancient watchtower or something, half buried in the sand, its windows dark with shadows. We pull up close to the stone wall, and my legs wobble as I slide down off the bike.

"Wait here."

Leif is a man of few words. Every sentence is clipped and to the point, his voice low and rumbling from the depths of his massive chest. It does something to me—that voice. It makes my body quiver to attention, like a tuning fork. I pivot to face him without thinking as he moves around, checking the tower is empty and safe.

After a minute, I remember myself, and jump to help, unpicking the knots he tied around my suitcase.

"Hannah." Leif's head sticks out of a tower window. "It's clear. You'll have to climb in this way." I look past him at the door, but it's halfway buried in sand. I don't even want to *think* about trying to dig it out of these shifting dunes.

"Okay." I grunt as my suitcase hits the ground. I drag it, puffing and grumbling to the window, to Leif's outstretched hand, a trail of sand rucking up under the wheels. As soon as it's in reach, Leif plucks my suitcase up like it weighs nothing, lifting it quickly through the open square of the window. I inch closer, chewing my lip. How to do this gracefully? But two hands close around my waist, lifting me up with a squeak.

I sail through the window, tucking my limbs, the air changing from a gentle breeze to stillness. The shadows are thicker inside, the darkness complete, and I grab a fistful of Leif's shirt when he lets go of my waist.

"Are you sure we should be in here?" I hiss. "What if it's cursed?"

I've seen Aladdin. I know how this goes. But Leif chuckles again, quiet and growly, and suddenly I'm glad he can't see the dopey smile on my face.

I don't know this man. I don't even trust him, not really. Not when my brain gets a word in over my traitorous body. But making him laugh somehow fills me with the biggest thrill; makes my toes curl in my sandals.

It's adrenaline. It must be. Our crazy circumstances making me feel silly things.

It's not *him*. Not us.

It can't be.

Leif

I brought her here to be safe. Against all my better judgement, I brought the hairdresser with me through the desert. I knew there would be others hunting her, but now that I've trapped her in this dark tower with me, the real danger becomes clear.

I can smell her. The tang of her sunscreen; the fruity scent of those oranges I watched her eat through my rifle scope. She's intoxicating, her scent filling the space without the desert breeze here to snatch it away. She's everywhere, in my nose, in my lungs, and my mouth waters as my cock swells harder against my thigh.

I've been some version of hard since I bundled her into my arms outside the tent. And driving the bike, her plump ass squeezed up against my lap, seeing her soft tits jiggle with every dip in the sand...

Forget it. She may be a hairdresser, but Hannah is the most dangerous woman of all.

"Do you have a flashlight?" She knocks into something in the dark, a dull thud echoing around the stone room. Her tiny hand is still clenched in my shirt.

Good. I never want her out of arm's reach again.

"One second." I dig through the backpack for my phone, switching on the flashlight app. It's blinding after a night of soft shadows, and bright spots burn in my eyes. I swing it around the edges of the round tower, over the drifts of sand and a half buried wood table and a shadowed pile against one wall—

"Oh god! Oh god! No! Nonononono…"

Hannah keep murmuring long after I toss the coiled snake through the window. It lands with a thump, stuck out there cold and damned to be motionless until the morning. If I'd been here alone, I'd let it have stay in the tower, but Hannah is still mumbling, an edge of panic in her voice.

"Be quiet." She glares at me but keeps freaking out, flapping her hands.

"Gross. Snakes. Gross."

"It's the Sahara. What did you expect?" I can't keep the bite from my tone, and she wilts in front of my eyes. She stops mumbling, but I suddenly wish she'd start up again. She seems so defeated now.

"You're right." She wraps her arms around her waist, giving herself a hug, and *god,* my heart squeezes so hard that I lose my breath. I step toward her, hands raised, but she turns away, staring at her case. "Um. What do we do now?"

"We sleep," I grind out. "Or you do, anyway. I'll wake you at dawn."

Hannah glances around the tower, the sand rising and falling in waves like the dunes outside, and I wait for her to complain. To say she needs a bed roll or something. But she nods, dragging her case against the wall and flopping down on the sand with her back against the luggage.

Her eyes dart around the room, searching for more creepy crawlies, and I wish I never snapped. She's clearly terrified.

"Okay. Um." God, I hate the false brightness to her voice. She never has to fake anything with me. "Goodnight, Leif. Sleep well."

I grunt. She shuffles until she's lying down, head pillowed awkwardly on the suitcase. Her breaths slow, her eyelids sealed closed, but she doesn't sleep. Not even after an hour. I know, because I'm watching her without blinking. With an unstoppable wave of obsession raging through my body. She's so dainty, so plump, so sweet, so guileless, and I want to see that pretty mouth open in pleasured cries.

Has she taken a man before? Has she touched herself, made herself come?

I groan and dig the heel of one palm into one eye.

I'm supposed to be keeping watch, but not like this. It's going to be a long night.

* * *

Two hours in, her breaths finally slow. They soften, dragging in and out of her chest, her pillowy tits rising and falling as she makes the cutest tiny snores. I fumble for my belt, self loathing thick in my throat, but I can't wait any longer. I need relief.

There are miles yet through the Sahara before we get back to safety. Miles of that dirt bike and her ass pressed against my cock. I'll never make it with my sanity intact—not without taking the edge off while I have the chance.

I'm already hard. I have been for hours. So hard I don't

remember how it feels to be soft. I draw my cock out with a hiss, tugging it roughly and swirling the pad of my thumb over the head. A bead of moisture gathers there, and I spread it around, stifling a groan as I screw my eyes shut.

Hannah's laugh. Her hair. The soft way she smiles in that photo of her; the way she bit my palm as I stole her away. The sights and sounds and sensations of Hannah rattle through me in a slideshow, and I pump my cock harder and faster with each remembered glimpse. I'm so caught up in my thoughts of her, in picturing her cupid's bow mouth sealed around my cock, that I don't register the shocked intake of breath until too late.

"Leif?" Her voice is rough from her stolen minutes of sleep. Hannah props herself up on her elbow, eyes wide as saucers as she stares at my cock. And I'm a monster, as bad as I've always feared, because I don't stop. I groan and pump my cock harder.

"Almost done, angel," I grit out. "Nearly done. Look away."

She doesn't listen. Her breath hitches, and god help me, she shuffles closer. This sweet, innocent girl with her big baby blues, she crawls over the sand to get a better look at my cock. It's flushed red and angry, harder than stone, and I clench my jaw as I tug it roughly, punishing myself for this.

"Does that feel good?" Hannah whispers. Her eyes dart up to mine, then back down. Her hands ball into fists, resting on top of her thighs.

"Yeah." I swirl my thumb over the head again. "Yeah." *Tug, tug.* "It feels good."

Hannah licks her lips. She shimmies closer again, and fuck, her *scent.* It drives me wild. Makes me grip my cock so hard that it throbs.

"Can I—can I touch it?"

My hand stutters. My rhythm slows as I stare at her, still dragging my fist up and down my thick length.

"Touch it?" I sound rough. Dangerous. "You want to touch my cock, angel?"

She bites her lip. And nods.

I'm on her before she can say another word. Before she can change her sweet mind. I scoop her up, placing her in my lap, and catch her soft, pale hand in my own. When her fingers wrap around my cock, guided by my own, the sound I make is *wounded*. Feral.

"Touch it," I rasp. "Play with it, angel. Whatever you want to do with it. It's yours."

Hannah

I've got myself into something. Something I don't understand. But, oh god, I *want* to. Leif's gray eyes are leveled on me, watching me closely, his hand urging me to stroke his thick length. He's searing hot under my palm, the skin sliding like silk, and moisture pools between my legs in response.

The thought of him inside me... that thick, full feeling...

I can't breathe.

"Easy, angel." His hand slows around mine. "Do you want to stop?"

"N-no." I squeeze him and he grunts. The hard muscles of his thighs practically vibrate with tension under my lap, and I start to rock aimlessly as I stroke him. I need something. Friction. *Something.*

"What do you need, angel?" It's like he can read my mind. I search for the words, but I don't know. *I don't know.* All I know is my insides are ratcheting tighter, tighter, and if I don't find some relief I might scream.

"I don't... I can't... *Leif.*"

"I've got you, baby. You want me to make you feel good?"

I nod, breath hiccuping out as I stroke his cock. This is supposed to be about him, but he plucks my hand away, scooping me up against his chest. He pushes to his feet, so fast I get vertigo, but then he's pushing me against the stone wall and I let out a blissful sigh.

Yes. This is what I want. To be pressed between Leif's hard chest and the cool tower wall. To feel him everywhere, to smell him, to feel his bare cock prod my core through the folds of my skirt.

"I'm a dangerous man," he murmurs. hips rocking against me. "I kill people. Do you understand that, Hannah?"

"Yes," I sob, scrabbling to grip his shoulders. He's so solid, so bulky, so intense.

"And do you think I might hurt you? Are you scared of me, angel?"

"No," I wail as his cock rubs over my clit through the thin fabric. "I'm n-not scared." It's barely anything, a brush of friction, but I nearly die on the spot. My pussy is wanting, clenching, desperate for him, and it's making me writhe in his grip. Making me rock my hips to meet him.

I want... I want...

"*Hannah.*" It's a warning. A prayer. "Do you want me to make you come?"

"*Yes,*" I hiss, and just like that he puts me down. I blink, arms suddenly empty, but then he's kneeling on the sand, his warm, callused palms sliding up the bare skin of my legs. My skirt gathers on his forearms as he goes higher, higher, and I splutter out a giggle as he hooks one of my legs over his shoulder.

"What's funny?" His mouth tugs at the corner as he slides his arms higher.

"This is. You are." I grab another fistful of shirt, thumping his shoulder. "I can't believe you're down there. On the floor."

"Oh, Hannah." His hands slide to the outside of my hips, and strong fingers hook the waistband of my panties. With one sharp tug, they tear away and flutter to the sand. "Get used to this sight, angel. For a girl like you, the world should fall to its knees."

I don't want *the world* on its knees, I want Leif. His cropped black hair and his piercing eyes. The way they crinkle at the edges as he smiles up at me, something unreadable swirling in their depths. I should be embarrassed, having my leg slung over him, heavy and plump. He can probably see my candy pink panties.

I'm not embarrassed. I'm so excited, I can hardly catch my breath.

"What are you going to do?"

"I'm going to touch you." A broad finger grazes my slit. "Tease you with my fingers. Make you whimper and beg. And when your legs are shaking, when you can barely stand up, I'm going to lick your pussy until you scream."

"People might hear," I manage, swaying in his hold. "People in the desert."

"They'll think we're ghosts. The spirits of long dead lovers."

It's a surprisingly beautiful thing for Leif to say. My mouth parts in shock, and I blink down at him, tongue-tied. Have I ever been tongue-tied before in my whole life? I don't think so.

"Shall we begin?" Leif's finger traces back and forth over the seam of my pussy, so gentle that he doesn't part my folds. It's barely a touch, barely anything, but I'm already on fire, and I nod so hard my teeth rattle in my skull. Leif chuckles, the sound rich with promise, then slides his finger harder along my pussy.

"Oh, gosh." I grip his shirt tighter, my head thumping back against the stone wall. "Oh, gosh. Leif."

"Mm?" He's knuckle-deep in me now, exploring me at a leisurely pace. His eyes glitter up at me as he swoops up to my clit, circling the tight bundle of nerves. "What is it, angel?"

"Don't..." I pant, squeezing my eyes shut. "Don't stop."

He hums, amused. "I won't. You'd have to tear me away."

His finger feels so different against my damp pussy. So much bigger and broader and more callused than my own fingertips, whenever I've explored down there before. Just that contrast—his masculine hands, intruding on my delicate flesh—it makes my blood sing.

Leif touches me slowly at first. Easing me into it. Then as my breath quickens and my cheeks flame brighter, his movements get rougher too. He strokes along my seam, firm and confident, and when I finally peel my eyes open and look down, he smirks and slides a fingertip into my entrance.

Just the tip. Up the the first knuckle. But already, I see stars. I rock my hips as much as I can on one leg, whimpering and urging him deeper. Leif obliges, sliding to the second knuckle, and I moan as loud as the wind through the dunes.

"You like that, angel?"

"Yes." I shake my handful of his shirt. "More."

"So demanding." Amusement curls through the words. Leif has a slight accent, a Norwegian lilt to his deep voice, and I love every sound that comes out of his mouth. I want to record him. Have him read my favorite books to me.

His finger pushes all the way in, stroking at my walls, and I clench down on him, helpless.

"Oh god. *Leif.*" If this is his finger, just a single finger.... the image of that thick cock I stroked not long ago flashes through my mind. Already, my pussy is stretching, the muscles burning at his intrusion. If I tried to get *that* inside me...

Would it even fit?

"What are you frowning about?" he murmurs, his finger sawing gently in and out. With every pass, he crooks his finger, stroking over a sensitive spot, and heat flares in my core. The ratchet twists tighter.

"I'm thinking..." I shake my head, trying to force myself to concentrate. To string a whole sentence together. "I'm worried about your—your cock."

Leif tilts his head, bemused. "I assure you, my cock is fine."

"No. No, I mean I'm worried about it fitting. In me."

"Ah." The sound rushes out of him like a sigh. Then the corner of his mouth tugs up. "It will fit, angel. If you want me inside you, nothing in this world could keep me out."

That sounds like kind of a painful promise. I'm really not sure. It's not that I'm a wimp, exactly—except yes, okay, I *am* a wimp. I cry when I stub my toe. When I got my shots for this vacation, I had to squeeze my eyes shut and pretend I was somewhere else.

I don't want to do that with Leif. Isn't the whole point to... be in the moment?

"Stop worrying," Leif orders, and despite myself, a sense of calm settles over my shoulders. "Do you trust me, angel?"

I nod.

"Good. Because I won't hurt you. I'll only ever make you feel good things." As if to demonstrate his point, Leif swirls his thumb over my clit at the same time that his finger plunges deep. My breath catches and he takes that as his cue, surging forward to lick a stripe up my pussy. His tongue is hot and wet, molding to my folds, and *god*, if this is what this feels like, why does anyone ever do anything else? Leif laps at me like a starving man, his groans vibrating through my flesh, and then my core is hot and tight and shuddering against his fingers, and a wave of pleasure washes through me from head to toe. I squeak, clinging to his shoulders for balance as I come and come and come.

Finally, I slump back against the stone wall.

"Oh," I manage. "Okay, that's... *oh.*"

Leif places my foot gently back on the ground and pushes to his feet. He looms over me, blocking out the muted starlight, and tugs his cock with rough, hurried motions as the other hand holds my skirt bundled at my waist.

Something warm and wet splashes over my bare legs. A drop lands right on the seam of my pussy.

"Fuck," Leif groans. "*Fuck.* Angel. Tell me you're mine."

"I'm yours," I breathe, peering up into his shadowed face. Leif says nothing for a long moment, his breaths harsh, then he uses the hem of my skirt to wipe the mess off thighs.

"Sorry," he grunts.

"It's okay. I have more clothes in my suitcase."

He snorts. "I bet you do."

We hover there, something fragile and confusing stretching between us. Then Leif turns away, and the moment's gone. I watch the shadowed bulk of him move away in the gloom, my heart sinking in my chest.

Was it not special for him the way it was for me? Does he do this kind of thing all the time with women he meets in the desert? I gnaw on my lip as I watch him, body slumped and cooling against the tower wall.

"Get some sleep," is all he says. And we're back to gruff orders and cool distance, like nothing ever happened, like he didn't just turn me inside out and bare all my secret longings to the night air. Tears burn at the back of my eyes, but I don't sniffle. Don't let him know. I cross to my suitcase, stumbling over the uneven sand, drop to the ground, and lie facing the wall.

I won't show him that he's hurt me. He never promised me anything, and besides—he's a dangerous man. We're from different worlds.

This is for the best, I tell myself, but I still don't sleep. I spend the rest of the night with eyes wide, staring at the stone.

Leif

There's something wrong with Hannah. Something besides being hunted by a hitman due to a case of mistaken identity. Yesterday, she was wary with me, nervous about her situation, sure, but her sparkle never dimmed.

Her light has gone out. She lies facing the wall until dawn, never falling asleep, but she doesn't say a word to me either. And when daylight spills through the tower's stone windows, she gets up before I can say anything, brushing the sand off her long skirt.

She digs through her suitcase, her back to me. Only glances back when she's ready to change.

I avert my eyes.

Did I do this somehow? Does she regret letting me touch her? Just the thought of that makes me want to howl at the sky. I strain to hear her as she shuffles around, packing up that monstrous case, but my chatty girl has gone quiet. There are no bright observations, no halting questions, no sweet giggles.

God. I should have left her at the tent.

But no—she wasn't safe there. And that's the most important thing. The *only* important thing. She can hate me if she needs to. Even though it cracks my chest open, chafes my heart raw, she can fear me. I'll still protect her. Now that I've touched her, *tasted* her, she's mine.

Mine.

"Quickly," I grumble. She huffs, and I hide a smile. When her suitcase wheels drag loudly through the sand, I turn and scoop the case up and stride to the window.

"Be careful!" Hannah rushes to my side just as I'm about to toss the case through to the ground. "My new hair straighteners. They're delicate."

This time I can't hide the grin stretching my cheeks. I lean over, lowering her suitcase carefully to the sand, then turn and grip her soft waist. She tenses under my hands, but lets me lift her through, too.

"No warning that time?" I ask, climbing through after her. "Are you not delicate, angel?"

"No," she snaps, marching to the bike. "I'm not."

She throws herself down on the seat, the bike rocking under her weight. I lash the suitcase on behind her, jaw clenched and mind racing, as she huffs and puffs and sighs.

"What is it?" I say finally, climbing on behind her. "What's got you so angry with me?"

With my thighs pressed against her legs, my arms caged around her body, the tension eases slightly in my chest. She's wearing a pair of cut-off denim shorts, the edges frayed, and those soft thighs are doing things to me. Wrapping an arm around her waist, I pull her flush back against me and show her firsthand the effect she has on me.

Hannah gasps, wriggling against the hard length pressed

against her back. See, even pissed off, she can't deny the pull between us.

"Nothing." She lets out a shuddery breath. "I'm not mad."

"Then prove it. Smile for me, angel." Her shoulders tense for a second, and I want to knead away those knots, but Hannah turns and flashes me those baby blues. Her mouth curves into a grudging smile, and my heart slams against my rib cage.

"There you are. Beautiful."

A pink blush creeps over her cheeks. And maybe it's me, or maybe it's the desert heat—the searing hot sun that's already baking the sand dunes. The heat is so intense, it shimmers in the air. You can almost hear it, tinkling on the edge of hearing like breaking glass.

I need to get her out of this. To safety and to shade. Enough messing around and flirting.

"Hold on tight." I reach around her for the handlebars. The dirt bike splutters to life. "We're not stopping until you're safe on a plane."

* * *

The gun shot cracks through the dunes. I curse and wrench the bike to the left, patting frantically at Hannah's body. She's not harmed—just shocked and confused, elbowing me in the gut as she tries to spin and look behind us.

"Get down!" I wrestle her back down, sheltered behind my bulk. If anyone wants to hurt her, they'll have to go through me.

"Who is it? What was that noise?"

"What do you think?" I snap. I'm too on edge to be nice, my teeth gritted so hard they might crack. Adrenaline courses through my limbs, turning my grip to iron as I wrench the dirt bike left and right. It wobbles like a drunken frat boy, the worst getaway vehicle I've ever used, its wheels spinning in the sand.

"Leif!" Hannah shrieks, then a body hurls off a dune, tackling us off the bike. Hannah flies out of my grip, and a roar bursts from my throat as I catch a glint of steel.

It's over before it began. I stand over the body, chest heaving, staring at the sickly angle of the man's broken neck. I don't recognize him, but even if I did, even if we'd been close friends, I wouldn't have hesitated.

No one touches Hannah. *No one.* I'll kill anyone who tries. And she must sense that blood lust in me, must see the vicious satisfaction in my face, because she staggers back three steps.

"Stop." She stumbles to a halt. Her eyes on me are wide and fearful. "Stay close. There might be others."

At least she doesn't run. I have this ounce of trust if nothing else—she'd rather risk spending more time with me than try her luck alone in the desert.

It takes ten minutes to hide the body. I dig a shallow ditch in the sand, then push it in and cover it back over. But when we climb back on the bike, Hannah tucked against my chest, she's so rigid I'm surprised she can bend her legs.

I should reassure her. Promise her she has nothing to fear—not from these others, and *never* from me. But if she doesn't know that already after last night, if she can't read my devotion in every word I utter, in every single thing I do...

Nothing I say will convince her.

I pull away without another word.

Hannah

I've never heard a gun shot before. It's silly, since I live in a big city, but honestly I'm kind of a homebody. I don't spend much time *out there*, where gun shots might be heard. I like movie nights in with friends and painting my nails on the sofa.

That thunder crack... the hard glint in Leif's eyes when he snapped that man's neck...

I swallow hard.

Leif doesn't say another word as we drive through the dunes. He's tense, on edge, his watchful gaze scanning the landscape, but he's distant too. And when we finally reach the edge of the dunes, the bike's wheels lurching up onto a road, he still says nothing.

Maybe he's tired of me. Counting down the minutes until I'm gone. And he definitely keeps talking about leaving me in the city—safe, yes, but away from *him*.

I'm starting to think I'll never be safe without Leif. Without him... my heart might break.

God. It's so silly. I'm a freaking hairdresser, and he's a

hitman. We're from different worlds. But when he touched me last night, when he dropped to his knees at my feet, a part of me thought that maybe... maybe I could keep him.

It's stupid. Such a *Hannah* thing to think. What am I gonna do, curl up with Leif on my tiny sofa? Make him blow on my nails until the polish dries?

"It's not far from here," Leif rumbles in my ear. "A few hours' drive until we reach the city."

"Then the airport," I murmur, icy numbness spreading through my tummy.

"Then the airport," Leif agrees.

* * *

He sweeps the terminal three times before he lets me go further than the coffee shop. The whole time, he makes me sit on the phone with him, chattering in his ear about any old nonsense so that he knows I'm alright.

"How do you even check for hitmen?" I muse as I watch his bulky form prowl between the check in desks. He's on the other side of the room, with crowds of tourists between us, but even from here I can see the power radiating from his every step. "Do you get taught that in assassin school?"

He laughs quietly, and I smirk down at my coffee. Leif insisted on paying, even though I still have almost all of my vacation money to spend. He even got me an extra shot of caramel and asked for chocolate sprinkles on the foam. The barista looked so freaked out, processing such a frivolous order for a grumpy mountain of a man.

"You look for people who are out of place. Ducking inside rooms they shouldn't; lingering too long even though they don't have luggage."

"Lots of people travel light these days."

"Do they?" Leif snorts. "I'm surprised you noticed. If that suitcase of yours falls off the luggage belt, it'll leave a crater in the tiles."

I grin, kicking my heels against the legs of my chair. Now and then, I remember the seriousness of my situation. I duck my head, hiding my face in my hair, and peer through the blonde strands for any signs of danger. But with Leif's voice in my ear, talking as easily as if we'd known each other for years, it's hard to be frightened. I know he's close.

"How's your coffee?" Leif asks suddenly. I take a sip, humming and licking sweet foam off my lip. "God," he mutters, so quiet I nearly miss it. "You're the real danger in this building."

Warmth spreads through my chest, so tickly and delicious, and I still have a goofy smile on my face when I leap to my feet.

"I've got an idea. Oh my gosh, this is genius. Just like in the movies."

"Hannah?" Leif's cool, calm tone is gone. He's urgent, and across the room he turns and cuts a path toward me through the crowd. "Wait there. Whatever it is, wait until I'm with you."

"I'm not a dumbass, Leif."

He mumbles something under his breath, and whatever it is, I'm one hundred percent sure he deserves the gray hairs I'm giving him. I wait like I'm told, draining the last mouthfuls of lukewarm coffee from my mug and wiping the stray foam onto my bare forearm. When he reaches me, eyes tight and worried, I spread my hands.

"Listen to this: hair dye."

Yep. I can actually see it: the exact moment that Leif snaps. Frustration and relief war on his surly face, and he rolls his eyes so hard, I'm surprised they don't get stuck in the back of his skull.

"This is not the time for a hairdresser moment, Hannah."

"No? You don't think changing my appearance will help *at all*, Sherlock?"

I love the grudging way he softens. The reluctant curl to his mouth. The days in the desert are showing on his tanned face, with stubble coating his strong jaw. I want to buff my nails on that stubble. I want to chafe my palms on it and listen for the rasp.

"Make it quick," he mutters, shaking his head as I whoop and tuck my hand in his arm. I steer him toward the open shop next to the check in desks, filled with shelves stacked with endless toiletries. "And nothing *cute*, Hannah. Pick a really different shade."

Oh, he has no idea. But he will soon.

Leif is going to dye my hair.

Leif

Is washing someone's hair always this fucking erotic? Hannah shivers with every scratch of my fingertips over her scalp. She hums, the noise sinful, and by the time I'm rinsing the dye from her hair, I'm so hard in my pants I can barely see straight. It's a good thing we're locked away in an unused, private bathroom, because if anyone walked in on this, I'd be arrested.

"Tilt your head," I grumble. She complies, smiling sweetly, her eyes closed and her lashes dusting her cheeks. Her skin is flushed pink from all those hours in the sun, and the knowledge that she burned under my care makes me want to put a fist through the wall.

I had one fucking job. And now my angel has a sunburn.

"What's got your panties in a knot?"

I glare down at her, but Hannah's eyes are resolutely closed. She sits in a chair in front of the sink, head tilted back, and she makes no effort to hide how much she's enjoying this. Now and then, she nudges the toe of my boot with her sandal, or bites her lip and shifts on the chair.

Yeah. I'm not the only one turned on by this.

Does that mean she gets worked up like this in her salon? Fuck. I'm jealous of strangers. I never want her to touch someone else's hair again.

"I don't like it," I mutter, since she's still waiting for an answer. Her pretty nose crinkles.

"The color?"

"No. Your job."

Those lashes flutter open, and she levels me a *look*. A look that chills me to the bone. I've seen less scary expressions on the other end of machetes.

"You don't like my job," she repeats flatly.

I swallow. "No." She opens her mouth to tear into me, her plump chest buoyed up by her rage, so I talk fast. "Not for good reasons. I know it's wrong. I just don't like the thought of you touching other people. This is…" I clear my throat, searching for the words. "It's *intimate*," I finish, voice hoarse.

Hannah softens beneath me, melting back against her chair. A calculating look flashes through her eyes, then her lids drop closed again. A faint smile tugs her lips.

"It's not usually like this." Something nudges my calf. A bare foot, slipped out of her sandal. It trails up the inside of my leg, burning a trail over my skin through the fabric. Hannah licks her lips, shifting again. "This is special."

Special. She's got that right. Hannah is the most *special* woman I've ever met. Every moment I spend with her is like a series of heart attacks, like getting a shot of electricity straight in my chest from one of those lifesaver machines. And the casual brush of her bare toes over the inside of my knee—that does more to me than entire nights spent with women in the past.

As if I could remember them anyway. Hannah has burned every other woman from my memory. She's a total eclipse.

Her breath shudders out of her chest on a sigh, and I can't stand it anymore. Can't loom over her like this without touching. I grunt, rinsing her newly red hair faster, but Hannah beats me to it. Her eyes flick open, steely determination setting her features, and she reaches for my belt buckle with steady hands.

"What are you doing, angel?" I rasp as she tugs my pants button open. She reaches in and pulls my hard length free, eyes widening as it bobs level with her chin.

"I'm returning the favor." Her hand is cool as it wraps around me, thanks to the overzealous air conditioning. I grit my teeth and hold her wrist in place, inwardly cursing myself to hell.

"Wait. Hannah. It wasn't a favor." I swallow and force the words out in a croak. "You don't owe me anything." It's true, and god knows I don't want her to ever do something for me out of obligation, but I still want to slam my head into the wall. Her presence in this small room is intoxicating—her scent, her body heat, every whisper of her clothes against her skin. If she really did put her mouth on my cock, I think I'd die and go to heaven right now.

Hannah shrugs. When she speaks, her voice is light. Casual. But I don't miss the hesitation in her eyes.

"I want it if you do."

"*Hannah.* I've never wanted something more."

Her first lick is cautious. Experimental. Like she's dining at a new restaurant and she's not sure yet if she trusts the chef. When an appreciate hum passes her lips, I about pass out with relief. And when she goes from zero to one hundred, from that tiny lick to sucking me down, I let out a strangled yell and stagger half a step forward.

116

"Hannah! Jesus Christ. Are you trying to suck out my soul?"

She moans and bobs her head, sucking me harder, and though I *know* she's never done this before, god, she's a fucking natural. Hannah was made to take my cock, the same way I was built to eat her sweet pussy. I groan and thrust gently—not enough to make her gag, but enough to urge her on. To show her what she's doing to me.

"Fuck. Yeah. That's right, baby. You're so good. Such a good girl." Hannah moans, her eyelids drooping as she squirms on her chair, her hand and mouth working me in tandem. And she looks so delicious, so flushed and needy, that I can't wait any longer. I ease her off gently, her lips releasing me with a wet pop.

"Angel." I crouch in front of her chair, running my shaking hands up her bare thighs. "Let me inside you. *Please.*"

It's so undignified, begging her like this, and though I'd never say those words for someone else, with her it feels right. It *is* a privilege to touch her, to taste her, and to bury my cock deep inside her—that would be the greatest gift of all.

Hannah sways on her chair, eyes glassy with arousal, and she wipes her wet chin on her forearm as she nods.

"Uh-huh," she hiccups, reaching for me with both arms. "I want that. I want it so bad, Leif."

"I've got you. I've got you." I don't know which of us I'm trying to soothe as I lift her into my arms. I turn us quickly in the cramped room, settling back down on the chair and placing Hannah on my lap. It's the same way she sat on me before, in the tower, as she pumped my cock in her sweet little hand. I thrust up against her now, rubbing along the seam of her shorts, and Hannah gasps and scrambles back to stand.

Disappointment punches my gut, but only for a split second.

117

Because then she's flicking her shorts button open and shimmying them down her hips. They drop to the bathroom tiles, followed quickly by her panties, and my angel is so worked up and needy that she doesn't bother to take anything else off. She climbs back into my lap with her tank top and one sandal on, the other kicked away somewhere on the floor. And she rises up, notching the broad head of my cock against her entrance before pausing. Meeting my eye.

"Like this?" she whispers, suddenly unsure. I take her waist in my hands and *squeeze*.

"Yeah, baby. Just like that."

She sinks down slowly. Inch by torturous inch, with tiny gasps as her inner muscles flutter and clench at the intrusion. I urge her to rise up and start again, the slickness of her pussy easing the way this time, and watch enraptured as the flush spreads from her cheeks, down her throat to her chest.

"Hannah," I groan, tugging her tank top and bra down, baring her nipples to the mercy of the air conditioning. They're pebbled, ready and wanting, and I seal my mouth over the left one and *suck*. She whimpers, rocking down another inch, and I knead her other tit in my palm.

"Wait." I raise my head in horror. I haven't even *kissed* her yet. It's such an awful oversight, so irredeemable, that my chest throbs as I cup her cheek. "Wait. This first."

She stills obediently, her hips twitching the tiniest bit as I coax her face toward mine. I hover with my lips a breath from hers, savoring the tension pulling taut between us. I can feel every one of her soft exhales on my lips. I can practically taste her sugary coffee already.

"You're mine, angel." I don't know where those words came from, but I will never take them back. "You're *mine*."

118

She nods, dazed, and her fingers clutch at my shirt. I can't bear it any longer. I slam my mouth onto hers.

It's a rough kiss. Bruising, *claiming,* with slanted mouths and deep, plunging tongues. Hannah gives as good as she gets, nipping at my lower lip and tugging me closer, closer, closer. Her hips begin to move again, sliding me deeper, and all I know in this moment is her perfect wet heat.

"God." I wrench my mouth away when I finally need to breathe, dropping my forehead onto her shoulder. Her newly red hairs tickle the side of my face, and how did I get here? How did I go from that shadowy, depressing strip club to this moment of pure, crystalline perfection?

"Leif." Her breaths are stuttered, ragged, and her thrusts against me become rougher as she gets used to the size of me. I'm the only man to be inside her, and that fills me with vicious, primal satisfaction. *No others,* a voice roars in my head. *No others but me.* I push it away, focusing instead on the snug clasp of her pussy, on her thump of her ass against my thighs, on the gorgeous little moans escaping her mouth. I pick up a handful of her hair, crushing it to my nose and breathing deep. I turn my face and lick a stripe up her neck.

She's mine. *Mine.* And I want to swallow her whole.

"Leif! I'm going to—I c-can't—"

I hush her, rubbing steady circles on her back. Her muscles twitch under my touch, every inch of her vibrating with tension, and I nip her earlobe as I murmur the words she needs to hear.

"Let it happen, angel. Come for me. I want you to come on my cock." I reach down between us, skating gentle circles on her clit to help her along, and Hannah lets out a shriek as she stiffens in my arms. She's fucking *magnificent* as she comes—unapologetic in the way she rocks harder, clamps down, tips her head back and *groans*.

"Oh. Oh my gosh." As soon as she's done, it's like her strings are cut. She slumps forward, arms looping around my neck, and buries her face in my throat. I hold her close as I thrust up into her once, twice more, then grit my teeth as my release surges up. I come harder than I ever have in my life, emptying my heart and soul up into this woman, and when I collapse back against the chair, we're both ruined.

We breathe together, chests rising and falling. Hannah squirms a little, then stills again, my softening cock still buried inside her.

"Angel?" I ask at last when I can form words again. "Are you alright?"

"Huh?" She sits up, hair mussed and face bright pink. She blows stray locks of hair out of her face. "Oh. Yeah. I'm—I'm alright. I'm *more* than alright. That was... incredible."

My chest swells, but I manage to choke back all the triumphant crowing. Instead, I smooth a hand over her damp hair.

"I'm glad."

We wait together in that tiny bathroom until our breathing is back to normal. Then we peel ourselves apart and start to clean up. And all the while, an icy cold dread snakes through my gut, chilling me from the inside.

I can't keep her. A man like me would never deserve her. Would be a source of danger. Would ruin her life.

But now I've touched her. Tasted her. Felt her from the inside.

How the hell am I supposed to let her go?

Hannah

He put me on the plane. I can't believe it. He really did put me on the plane.

When we came out of the bathroom, straightening our clothes and clearing our throats, Leif seemed fine. A bit quiet, maybe, but when is he not? Then he marched me to the ticket desk, a firm hand clamped on my elbow, and I knew. With my chest cracking open down the middle, I realized.

He still wanted to get rid of me.

It didn't matter that we just shared the most breathtaking experience of my life. That the minutes we spent gasping and clutching at each other, driven half out of our minds by need—they *changed* me. I can't go back.

I can never un-know how it feels to be loved by Leif.

Loved physically, anyway.

Because if there were any more to it, if he felt as tied up in knots over me as I do over him, he'd never buy a single ticket back to the US. He'd never guide me through the terminal, tripping over my own feet, too numb with horror to really process what's happening.

And he definitely wouldn't stand with his arms crossed in the departure lounge, scowling as I shuffle up in the boarding line. He waited until the last second, until I disappeared through the doorway, but in all that time he never even said goodbye.

So that's it. My big romance with the hitman. Over before it really began. And now I'm folded into a seat on this plane, forehead pressed to the window, trying and failing to catch my breath. I wrap my arms tight around my waist and hunch forward, like I can hold my heart in my body and stop it from spilling, ruined, onto the fuzzy carpet below my feet.

"You okay, honey?"

A kindly woman with wiry gray hair and a Texas drawl squeezes into the row in front of me. I nod up at her, forcing a strained smile, and she hums but says nothing more.

Perfect. I'm a mess for everyone to see.

The passengers file in like grumpy cattle, squeezing into the cramped seats and shoving their hand luggage in the racks overhead. My bright pink suitcase is somewhere in the belly of this plane, checked in by Leif back at the ticket desk. He did everything for me, so steady and careful, and even when my heart was breaking I felt so safe with him near.

Now he's gone. And I'm left with nothing except sunburned cheeks, an ache between my legs, and a ruined vacation. The thought of going back home after spending all that money and not even seeing the world, going back to the cold, windswept city and the salon I share with three other hairdressers...

I like my life. I know I'm lucky, and I'm grateful. But right now in this moment, I'd rather leap out of the plane. And isn't that awful, when I might still be in danger, all because I look like some crazy mob woman?

The air stewards line up in the aisle, pointing at emergency exits and miming how to blow a whistle. I stare at them numbly, too exhausted to think straight.

"Cheer up, honey." The Texas woman peers at me between the gap in the seats. "It can't be all bad."

No. No, it's not all bad. I got to see the Sahara; I had those precious stolen moments with Leif. And I'll be back, damn it. I won't hide forever. I'll save up again and visit another wonder of the world.

"You're right." I smile at her properly this time, gripping the arm rests as the plane rushes down the runway, tilting back as it leaves the tarmac. My stomach swoops, left behind for a second, and I squeeze my eyes shut. I hate this bit.

That's why I don't see the commotion. I only hear the shocked gasps; the shriek of the Texas woman. I squint one eye open and find a gun shoved in my face, a blank-faced man holding it out like he's offering me the newspaper.

"Viper," he says.

"Oh no, no, no," I moan, scrabbling to press myself back against the seat. The man cocks his head and adjusts his arm, his finger inching toward the trigger, but a dark shape rushes him, tackling him to the ground. Grunts and the thump of fists hitting flesh drift up from the aisle, and the air steward shrieks and hops up and down as the gun is tossed along the floor her way.

I don't have to wonder. I know who it is. I knew the second his shape moved in the corner of my eye. Leif would never leave me vulnerable, unprotected. Would never leave my survival to chance.

He subdues this assassin as easily as the last one, though he lets him live, stopping after breaking both arms. I guess because people are watching. He looks up then and winks at me, like he's reading my mind.

God. We've only been parted for thirty minutes, but my heart slams against my rib cage like it's been ten years. I mouth his name, too overwhelmed to speak, and he nods at me, face etched with regret.

It's okay. I rub a hand over my chest, willing my heart to calm down.

I know how he can make it up to me.

Leif

"You want me to paint your nails." I stare at Hannah, but she glares back at me, chin raised. She's still prickly with me, grumpy and hurt, even though it's been two days since I delivered her safely back home.

She watched me sweep her apartment, face pale and drawn, but when I shut the door behind us and stayed—she finally smiled.

Told me to sleep on the sofa, but hey. One step at a time.

I knew it was a mistake to leave her. The second she disappeared through that doorway leading to the plane, every atom in me screamed out to follow her. So I did, buying a ticket and racing to board in record time. I should have gone straight to her, but I was a coward.

I wanted time to rehearse my apology. My big speech declaring my love. And that hesitation nearly cost me everything. I never thought another professional would be so bold, so careless, but the Viper has made a lot of enemies. There are people who don't care what happens to them, as long as she dies.

I will never risk Hannah again. Never let her out of my sight. And if she wants me to paint her nails... well, someone pass me the brush.

"You know I'm going to mess them up, right?"

She clicks her tongue. "I thought hitmen have steady hands?"

"No part of me is steady around you."

It's true. My angel jangles me up without trying. One toss of her blonde-again hair and I'm ruined. I slide my palms up her legs now where they're tossed over my lap, but she shoves a bottle of turquoise nail polish into my hand instead.

She can't hide that shiver, though. My angel still wants me the way I want her. And no matter how long she makes me wait, whether it's weeks or months or years, I'll be here. Working to win her back.

"Wow, you are bad at this." I wince as I splodge a bit of varnish over her knuckle.

"Sorry. I'll look up a tutorial later. I'll get better."

Hannah snorts and swipes the bottle back out of my hand, scrubbing her knuckle with a wipe. Then she paints her nails, fast and flawless, and I watch her, absorbed.

"Blow." Her fingers hover inches from my lips. I blow on them gently, meeting her eyes. Letting her see every ounce of my devotion for her. My *hunger*.

Hannah is mine.

She shivers, wriggling on the sofa cushion. Pressing her thighs together. I grin, shark like, and catch her slender wrist, pressing a kiss to the delicate skin.

"Later," I growl, inhaling her scent and watching her blush. "Once your pretty nails have dried."

"Then what?" she asks, eyes glassy, squirming for friction,

and triumph roars through my chest. She's letting me back in. Letting me *prove* to her just how badly I need her.

"Then I'll pull these leggings down and bend you over the sofa, and fuck you until you forget your own name."

She's nodding already, gulping and eager, and I trail a hand up her thigh, tracing the inner seam of the fabric.

She can't touch me while her nails are wet. But that doesn't mean I can't touch *her.* And my angel should never be kept waiting.

I swore it. Never again.

Hannah

❦

Three years later

My husband is a scary man.

Not to *me,* obviously. Leif would slit his own throat before causing me to break a nail.

But to everyone else, he is a hulking presence. A burly wall of a man, filling doorways and blocking out the light, glowering at anyone who dares monopolize my time.

My best friends are used to him. They roll their eyes and tease him just like I do. But everyone else, especially the men that hang around me sometimes, hopeful looks on their faces...

Leif enjoys scaring the crap out of them.

"Be friendly," I hiss as we climb slowly down the rickety metal steps that jut out from the plane. "I want to meet people. Get to know the culture. I can't do that if you're murdering them with your eyes."

I'm finally abroad. Stepping into another country—Italy this time, with its ancient history and sumptuous food and sun-soaked beaches. It took three years until Leif was sure it was safe. Until we got word that someone *finally* took out the Viper.

A tiny part of me is almost sad that she's gone. We were weirdly connected, somehow. Then I remember how awful she was, how many lives she ruined, and how I've waited three years for another vacation.

Sayonara, Viper.

"Be careful," Leif mutters as I stumble on a wonky step. He's got one huge hand clamped on my shoulder, ready to pluck me into the air if it even *looks* like I might fall.

It should probably be annoying. Claustrophobic. But honestly? I feel treasured.

"Can we go to the Colosseum? And the Vatican? And all the art galleries? Can we get a proper pizza, from a tiny little side street restaurant? Can we—"

"We can do everything you like, angel." Leif sounds amused. "Just make sure you don't twist your ankle first."

He's always like this. Everyone thinks he's so surly, but he's super protective. *Nurturing.* And now more than ever, I'm glad for that fact. I smooth a hand over the bump growing under my loose white t-shirt. It won't be just the two of us for much longer. All the more reason to see the world now, to go on adventures—we've got a very different adventure coming down the line.

"Do you think the baby can tell we're here?"

Leif snorts. "Sure. I bet the baby already speaks Italian."

"Shut up," I mutter, but I shoot him a grin.

This is it. Everything I've been dreaming of. Adventure and romance and family and *fun.* And I get to do it all with a man who worships the ground I walk on. Who seems to think rubbing my feet after a long day at the salon is a privilege, not a chore.

A man who makes me scream every night, licking my pussy with single-minded purpose, practically possessed by the devil.

Yeah. I beam up at the bright sunshine.

It's going to be so much fun.

III

Ocean Jewel

Description

My older brother means the world to me. I owe him everything.

But if he knew the filthy daydreams I have of his best friend... he'd never look at me the same way.

Damian is steady. Rugged and manly. Tailor-made to make me sigh. So when my brother invites me on a sailing trip and says Damian will be there...

I can't resist. I need him near.

It's silly. Because when Damian looks at me, he still sees a little girl. So I'm stuck out on the ocean with only my sketchbook to console me, drawing us together as I wish it could be.

Desperate. Primal. Nothing between us but skin.

Except I'm careless with my sketchbook. I leave it lying around on deck. And soon Damian looks at me differently, too.

Like I'm forbidden.

But too tempting to resist.

Roxy

I stroll along the edge of the harbor, salt air whipping at my cheeks. Excitement bubbles in my chest as I hitch my backpack higher on my shoulders, the fabric straining with hastily stuffed clothes and arts supplies.

Two weeks on the water. Two whole weeks with my older brother Jake, the man who practically raised me. Who I've barely seen for the last six months.

And two weeks with *him*.

Jake's best friend. The man I'm not supposed to want. The man who's dominated my daydreams since I was a teenager.

Damian Flint.

Seabirds cackle and wheel overhead, the wind ruffling their white and gray feathers. I shield my eyes against the bright morning sun, scanning the boats bobbing against the jetty. Jake was rushed when he called me a few days ago, always being torn in all directions by work, but I *swear* he said 'sailing' trip.

I don't see any sails. Not on boats big enough for us to live on. The thought of the three of us squeezing onto one of these tiny clinking sailboats, Damian's hard chest pressed against my back… I clear my throat, fanning my cheeks.

Get it together, Roxy. He doesn't see me that way.

He never will.

"Roxy!" The cry is faint, the voice snatched away by the coastal wind. I turn and peer around the boats, scanning everything from battered fishing trawlers to compact luxury cruisers. "Over here!"

A glimpse of movement catches my eye: my brother waving his whole arm, standing backlit by the morning sun. I beam and start to run, my heavy bag thumping against my back.

Jake. I've missed my big brother so much.

Don't get me wrong, I'm happy for him. He's worked so hard for so long, and now that his documentary film-making career is finally taking off—I'm proud enough to burst. For the last six months since his big breakout film, he's barely slept in the apartment we share for a single night. His phone is constantly buzzing and pinging; he's lived out of a duffel bag for weeks on end. When he *does* tear through our apartment like a hurricane, I barely have time to hug him and shove a piece of toast in his hand before he's gone again.

Usually, I'm left behind when work calls him away on shoots. I'm nineteen, after all. I graduated high school last summer, and now it's time to figure out my own path. And if some nights our apartment is so full of echoes and shadows that I can't sleep… well, I'll get over it. I'll buy a night light or something. But *this* time, Jake called me from the airport, bursting with excitement for this next big project.

A documentary for a big name channel, all about people who choose to live offshore. And two weeks at sea, paid for by the channel. With room for Damian to come on as project manager, Jake said, so proud and excited. Damian, and little old me.

He didn't need to sell me the rest. My brother could have told me I'd be spending two weeks sleeping in a ditch, and I'd have gone if Damian would be there. Curled around me. Glancing at me with those dark eyes, his gaze lingering just a few seconds too long.

I shiver, biting my lip as I slow to a walk beside Jake's boat. It's big—some kind of expedition yacht. A sturdier, more rugged version than its luxury siblings. The metal sides loom out of the water, towering above me, and I have to tilt my head back to see the railings surrounding the top deck.

"Rox!" Jake clatters down a wooden plank, his face stretched into a goofy grin. He meets me in a few strides of his long legs, scooping me up in a hug and swinging me around, heavy backpack and all. I laugh, face squashed against his chest, the zipper of his sweater digging into my cheek.

"I missed you so much." He puts me down and ruffles my dark hair, messing it up even worse than the sea breeze. His hair is just as dark as mine, sticking up from the way he constantly drags his hands through it, and his jaw is dusted with stubble.

Behind him, a figure appears at the top of the ramp, strong arms crossed over a broad chest. My mouth runs dry. "I'm glad you're here, Rox. Now I can keep an eye on you." Jake winks, turning to call over his shoulder, "Right, man?"

"Right." Damian's voice is much calmer than Jake's as he strides down the ramp to the stone jetty. He's always been the steady force, anchoring Jake's creative chaos. Damian Flint is unflappable. Stern. The most solid man I've ever met.

I stare at him, heart skittering in my chest.

"Hello, Roxy." He smiles at me, polite but distant. Jake finds it hilarious, how formal Damian is with me. The way he never teases me, never lets the two of us be alone. Both men are in their thirties, but Jake still ribs him like they're in college. "How are you?"

I lick my lips, my voice coming out in a whisper. "I'm good, thank you."

This is the problem. My crush on Damian has been festering inside me since I first really looked at a man. It's a real, solid thing inside me: a heavy, dense lump that sits in my chest and crowds out my lungs. My pulse races at merely the thought of him. I flush hot when I hear only the timber of his voice.

So even though I'm a grown woman now, an adult trying to find her way in the world, Damian makes me feel like a stuttering teenager again.

A silly girl with a silly infatuation.

No one he could ever really want.

Jake snorts, slinging his arm around my shoulders, and guides me towards the boat. "You'll have to learn to talk to him soon, Rox." What is he doing? Damian can *hear him*. My cheeks flush crimson, and I fight the urge to push Jake off the jetty. "Two weeks is a long time to spend out there on the ocean. Just the three of us, the captain and the crew."

A thought seems to occur to Jake, crinkling his forehead, and he gives me a little shake. "Don't go cozying up to any of the crew, you hear?"

I steal a glance over at Damian and find his brown eyes already on me. He waits for my answer too, his jaw clenched shut, the morning sunshine glinting off gold strands of his dark blond hair.

"I won't," I promise, but I say it to *him.* Jake can huff and puff all he likes, but my brother doesn't own me. I'm a grown woman and I can make my own decisions.

Damian, on the other hand...

He doesn't own me either. But I sure do wish he'd try.

Damian

I've made an error in judgment. It's a rare occurrence, but this is a serious misstep. I should never have agreed to this job.

Because Roxy is here.

Oh, I knew she was coming. Jake went on and on about it, so excited to spend some time with his little sister, for her to see him in action on the job. And he was very clear about what her presence meant for me as project manager: Roxy was to have her own cabin, her sleeping quarters as far from the crew as physically possible. When he met me at the harbor at dawn, the first thing he asked me to show him was where his baby sister will be staying.

I put her in the cabin next to mine. Refused to let myself think about it too hard. To examine the dark, possessive feelings that curl in my gut whenever I think about Jake's sweet little sister.

"Awesome. Perfect. Yeah, thanks, man." Jake clapped me on the shoulder, relief on his smiling face. And guilt surged up the back of my throat, even as I nodded and showed him to his own cabin next, just a few feet down the cramped corridor. Our boots echoed on the metal floor, and Jake chattered on about his plans for the documentary, oblivious to the shame curdling in my chest.

I have no right putting her in the cabin next to mine.

That's not protection. That's testing my already wafer-thin control.

That's feeding her to the wolves.

When I accepted this job, I figured it wouldn't be so bad. Surely I must have exaggerated the effect she had on me the last time I saw her—after all, I only noticed Roxy at all in this way since she turned eighteen. Since she became a *woman*. And I've only seen her a handful of times since then, but each time has been like a three-hour heart attack.

Her big gray eyes. Those pillowy lips, parting on a sigh. Her long dark hair, sliding over her shoulders, just begging to be wound around my knuckles and *tugged*.

Roxy West needs to stay far away from me. I'm too old for her, too hardened by life. And worst of all, I'm her brother's best friend. This man is closer than family to me, and I owe him more loyalty than I'll ever be able to repay.

Instead, I hunger after his baby sister. I fist my cock in the shower every day and think of *her*.

It's a good thing no one can read these thoughts. If they could, I'd be back on the harbor with my bag thrown at my head faster than I could catch a breath.

I follow Roxy and Jake back on board now, prowling silently after them down the corridors. Jake points out the galley kitchen, the mess spaces, the bathrooms, the cabins. He repeats his warning about staying away from the crew, and I glimpse Roxy rolling her eyes as she turns away to look through a porthole.

I stifle a smirk, looking down at my boots.

She's not mine to smile at.

She's not my *anything*.

"You're sleeping next to Damian," Jake tells her, tugging her by the elbow down the corridor. She trips over her boots trying to keep up, and I grind my teeth to keep from barking at him to let her go.

He'd never hurt her. Jake would chop off a limb before he harmed his baby sister. Hell, he practically raised her, their parents ducking out of the picture as soon as their oldest child could stand on his own feet.

I still don't like him yanking her along like that. Doesn't matter *how* excited he is.

She's precious, damn it. Handle with care.

Roxy sucks in a shaky breath and glances at me over her shoulder. I wipe my face blank as she turns, giving a polite nod and gesturing for her to keep up. She turns away, hurrying after her brother.

"I don't—um. What?"

"Your cabin is next to Damian's." Jake grins proudly as we reach the door to her sleeping quarters. Roxy flushes pink, and I try not to think about what she *thought* he meant.

It's nothing. Probably nothing.

And her brother is *right there*, damn it.

"Am I sharing with anyone?" Roxy pokes her head through the doorway, little pleased sounds at her cabin floating back into the corridor. I close my eyes and pinch the bridge of my nose, willing the swelling in my jeans to go down.

"You alright?" Jake murmurs.

I drop my hand and nod. "Headache." I don't trust myself to

say any more. And I doubt I could if I tried—something about Roxy's presence makes me even more reluctant to talk than usual. My jaw is constantly clenched shut, my tongue glued to the roof of my mouth. Because if I let myself speak freely, if I said the things I long to say...

They'd both be horrified. And they'd be *right*.

"Of course you're not sharing." Jake follows Roxy into her cabin, their voices bouncing off all the metal and wood in the corridor. "You think I trust anyone with my baby sister?"

"What about Damian?" Roxy murmurs. I turn to stone, straining to hear his reply.

"He doesn't count." I can practically see Jake wave a hand. "That's why his cabin is next door."

Roxy hums in agreement, and suddenly I don't want to hear any more. I turn on my heel without saying another word, striding back along the corridor to find the captain. I've got work to do. This is—this is a distraction.

Nothing more.

I rub a palm over my chest as I walk, eyes fixed unblinking on the stairs to the upper deck. I clatter up those metal steps, thighs bunching, and don't breathe easy until I'm out in the fresh salt air.

This was a mistake. But it's just two weeks.

Two weeks.

I can avoid her for that long.

Roxy

When I was in high school, Damian used to crash at our place on some nights. Our apartment is small—cozy, as Jake puts it—with nowhere for a guest to stay except the couch. But Damian lives out of the city, no doubt in some manly retreat in the mountains, so on days when he lingered long after dark, he'd crash for the night instead of drive home late.

Jake told him he was always welcome. Damian still asked my permission every single time. I told him Jake said it was okay, and Damian smiled at me and said it was my home too.

That was the start of it, I think. Those little generous moments, when he asked what I thought and really waited for the answer. I was still a gawky school girl, coltish and not fleshed out yet. And I was so freaking nervous around him, always stuttering and forgetting my words.

Knowing he was out there, a single bedroom door separating us at night...

He'd never shown any interest. He looked at me with kindness, but that was all. I knew surer than I knew my own name, that if I tiptoed out there, if I told him how much I loved him—he'd be horrified.

So I never told him. I never spoke my crush out loud, even though every night he spent in our shadowy apartment, the longing grew so fierce it was almost too much to bear. My crush grew heavier inside me, squashing my lungs and stealing my breath, and as I matured, it took on a new darkness.

I didn't just want the kind, smiling Damian. I wanted his gruff, moody side too. The side Jake teased whenever it came out, but that made goosebumps ripple down my arms.

The night after my high school graduation, Damian happened to crash at our place. And I lay in my bedroom, so close to him I could hear his steady breaths through the door, and touched myself. I imagined that it was *his* hands smoothing over my bare stomach, his fingers pinching my nipple. Dipping into my core.

I touched myself the way I thought Damian might touch me. Rough and urgent and wild. With all the pent up frustration he never lets anyone see. Anyone but me, and only because I watch him when no one else does.

Since Jake has been crazy busy with work, Damian has stopped coming too. There's no draw for him now, after all—now that it's only me at home. He came knocking one night early on, and I invited him inside anyway.

Damian shook his head so firmly, I'm surprised his neck didn't snap.

I told myself that it was okay. That it made perfect sense that Damian didn't want to see me, only Jake. That it didn't hurt me *that* badly—my raw, sandpaper heart was because I missed my brother too.

That's all.

Still, I'm not prepared to finally sleep one wall away from Damian again. I sit in my narrow bed—more of a cot than anything—and chew on my lip, staring at the wall I'll share with Damian for two whole weeks. The boat rocks gently in the harbor waves, the crew shouting to each other up on deck. We're heading off soon, out into the ocean, and then it's too late to turn back. To think better of this. And maybe I have awful self-preservation, but the thought of leaving now—it's impossible.

It doesn't matter how much it hurts. How much it tightens my chest and makes my heart throb.

I need to be near him. It's been so long since I heard his low breaths through the wall.

The boat lurches to one side, the rumble of an engine vibrating through the floor, and I grab the bed covers for balance. My backpack crashes to the floor, tangled clothes and sketchpads and pencils exploding everywhere, and I let out a cry before dropping to my knees. I don't care about the clothes—I didn't even fold them—but my *art supplies*—

The door to my cabin crashes open. Damian stands in the gap, a scowl etched on his face and his chest heaving. I blink up at him from my knees, a sketchpad in one hand and a box of charcoals in the other.

He scans my body, frowning. Peers around the cabin.

"I heard a noise. Did you fall—"

"No." My voice comes out in a squeak. I raise the box of charcoals, rattling the contents uselessly. "My stuff fell off the bed."

He huffs, something flickering in his expression, but Damian steps inside my tiny cabin and crouches beside me. He gathers my things quickly, placing them back in my bag with care, his hands so much *bigger* than mine. Able to grip twice, three times as much.

I picture those big hands on my body. Squeezing my hip; kneading my breast. I whimper, shifting on my knees.

Damian glances at me quickly, his eyes raking over my body then away. A muscle tics in his jaw.

"And you're not hurt?" he asks quietly.

I shake my head, my throat too tight to speak. Damian nods once, curt, then pushes to his feet and places my repacked bag on my bed. When he straightens up, he fills almost every inch of spare space in my cabin. It's a tiny room—just a cot and a shelf with a string across it to keep books from falling. A closet fixed to the wall, smaller even than me, and a porthole, showing off the sparkling waves.

"Be careful," he mutters. "We're about to pull away. It's only going to get rougher."

I manage to nod, unsticking my tongue to whisper, "Thank you." But he's already gone. The rhythmic thud of his boots echoes back through my cracked doorway, and I stare after him with ringing in my ears.

I've made a mistake. Two weeks with Damian?

I'll never keep my crush secret that long.

* * *

As soon as we're out of the harbor, Jake gets to work. He sets up shots of the shrinking shoreline; gets footage of the whole boat; interviews the captain and half the crew. He's in filmmaker mode, which means he won't resurface now until his body is on the brink of collapse. Only then will he let me shove a bowl of food into his hands before he crashes into fitful sleep. Then he'll wake up and do it all again.

I'm happy for my brother. He's found his passion, and what's more, he's *great* at it. So brimming with talent that people line up to work with him.

But I'd be lying if I said I'm not a teensy bit jealous. Of his passion; his single-minded direction; of every second of his time. All of it. Here I am, halfway through the year out I took to figure out my next steps, and I still have no more clue than six months ago.

Only some half-filled art school applications that make my stomach flip when I think about them.

I push all those ugly feelings down and carry a sketchpad and two pencils up to the deck. I'm bundled up in a padded coat, but even with the thick, downy layer, the icy breeze still steals my breath. I blow on my knuckles as I wander around the railings, searching for the perfect place to sit. Somewhere sturdy and sheltered, with good views to draw.

That part is easy. *Every* view here is breathtaking, whether it's the majestic boat bearing us into the ocean, or the silvery waves, getting rougher the further we get from the shore.

"Drawing?" Just his low voice—just that one word—makes me shiver. I turn and find Damian in the shadows, arms crossed as he watches me.

"Uh-huh." I raise the sketchpad like an idiot. "I, um. I love to draw."

I love to draw? Kill me. Someone throw me overboard. What is it about this man that turns me into a complete fool? Not only is that fact really freaking obvious by the art supplies I'm carrying, Damian has seen plenty of my work firsthand. Jake has an embarrassing habit of displaying my sketches and paintings in our apartment, even buying special frames for them.

"I know." The corner of Damian's mouth ticks up. "Might be a challenge. The trip will be rocky."

I nod again and escape, fleeing to the other side of the deck and clambering up onto a flat surface out of the worst of the breeze.

This trip will be rocky?

He has no idea.

Damian

The lights below deck cast more shadows than they illuminate. I prowl through the corridors after dinner, too restless to stand up on deck and watch the stars without knowing exactly where Roxy is. She slipped away after eating, excusing herself in that sweet little whisper, and I haven't seen her since.

I'm just checking on her. Taking care of her, like Jake wants. *Not exactly like Jake wants,* a voice whispers in my head, but I ignore it. If my best friend knew all the ways I want to *take care* of his little sister, he'd punch me in the face.

I'd let him. There's no excuse.

Our three cabins are down their own corridor: first Jake's, then a few strides later, mine and Roxy's, clustered together at the end. I should have put Jake next to her. I *know* I should have. And he trusts me so well, he didn't even question it.

I groan and dig the heel of my palm into one eye, coming to a stop outside Roxy's door. I raise a fist, then lower it. Suck in a sharp breath through my nose. Hold it until it gusts out in one go. Then raise my fist again and knock this time.

Nothing. Her cabin is silent. There's no creak of the floor; no sounds of rummaging or rolling over in bed.

She's not there.

Panic crowds my skull, white-hot and overwhelming, but I don't have time to do anything before soft footsteps round the corner. I spin on my heel and gape at the sight before me—Roxy padding under the weak lights, nothing but a towel wrapped around her wet body. Wisps of steam rise off her flushed skin, beads of water slide down her shoulders from her wet hair, and she gives me a shy smile as she approaches.

"Roxy." My word cracks through the quiet. The smile drops off her sweet face. "What the hell are you doing?"

A tiny line creases her forehead. Her cheeks flush pink, but she raises her chin and meets my eyes. Those pale gray irises send shock waves through my chest.

I've rattled her.

She comes to a stop in front of her cabin, but she doesn't reach for the door. And-and I'm in her way, blocking the door, so I clear my throat as I step to the side.

"I took a shower." Her words are quiet but fierce. "Is there something wrong with that?"

"*Yes.*" Screw giving her space. I crowd back in closer, rubbing the corner of her towel between my thumb and finger. One swift tug, and it would drop to the floor. "This boat is full of crew. Strangers. Men who'll take a single look at your perfect body and your flimsy towel and take it as an invitation to stare."

I can't stop looking at her, like I need to demonstrate my point. I've thought of her naked so many times, hating myself for every second of it, but I've never been able to fill in the details.

Right now, there's still a towel in the way, but I can see so much more than ever before. The gentle slope of her shoulders; the soft swell of her breasts; the line of her thighs beneath the far-too-short hem. I soak up every detail like a starving man, but behind the lust, there's something else.

Jealousy. Bitterness. If I can see this, others can too.

And she's *mine.* Mine to stare at. Mine to unwrap like a birthday gift. Except-except *no,* she's not, and I force myself to step back with every last ounce of my willpower. I let the corner of her towel drop, forcing my grip open like it's the hardest thing I've ever done. Roxy watches me go, mouth parted and pupils blown wide, and I've never been so hard in my whole goddamn life.

Can she tell? Can she see how ravenous she makes me; how I'm two seconds from snapping and throwing her over my shoulder?

I reach past her and shove her cabin door open.

"Get inside."

Roxy huffs, bundling her towel tighter around her, and stays put. I take her by the elbow, intending to steer her inside, but that warm, damp skin beneath my palm does something to me. I hiss, stepping closer again, my thumb tracing over her arm in circles.

"What's going on?" Jake's voice echoes down the corridor. We leap apart, eyes wide and chests heaving. I'm the first to recover, meeting Jake's eyes and smirking as he walks to join us. He's never looked at me like that—with a hint of suspicion swirling in his gaze—and I *hate* it.

"Roxy here is out to tempt the crew."

She sucks in a breath, outraged, and gives me such a look of hurt and betrayal that I wish I could snatch the words back.

I'm being an asshole, blaming her for my own primal reaction, and now I'm shoving all the awkwardness I'm feeling onto her shoulders. I open my mouth to put it right somehow, to take my share of the blame, but Jake booms out a laugh, tired but amused.

"Come on, sis. You know better than that."

She throws us both a disgusted look. "You're right. I do." It's the firmest her voice has ever sounded around me, and I'm not sure I like that. There's a hard edge to her words, a cool distance in her eyes when she glances at me one last time before stepping into her cabin.

She shuts the door without another word, and I want more than anything to pound on it until she listens to me. Until she lets me apologize.

Until she lets me peel that goddamn towel off her beautiful curves.

I don't do it. I *can't*. Not with her brother right here—and it would be wrong anyway.

She's young. Sweet. Too good for me by far. It's not her fault that she doesn't know what effect she has on me—what a torment her bare skin presents. And why would she? Roxy trusts me. Or she did, until I threw her under the bus.

"Come back to the galley." Jake claps me on the shoulder, all hints of suspicion long gone. "We need to go over the schedule."

Of course. This is a work trip. I have a job to do, and it does not involve snapping at his baby sister's heels. We're on tight deadlines, with a trail of boats we've arranged to meet with out in the ocean so Jake can film the occupants.

I can't afford these distractions. I can't afford *her*.

Not when she makes me want to throw all the rest of it away.

I knock on Roxy's cabin door long after her brother is asleep. I know, because I ply him with whisky, bastard that I am. Not enough to get him drunk or even tipsy, but enough that he'll let the work stuff go for a half a minute and let me usher him back to his cabin. His eyelids are drooping, his face already hollowed with exhaustion, and worry for him gnaws at my gut.

I've always taken care of Jake. Even when we were teenagers ourselves, we had each other's backs, but Jake always managed to get himself in more scrapes. And I'd be the one to swoop in and fix things, to set things right and clean up his mess. He's grateful, I know he is, and hell—I've made a whole career since out of being a *fixer*.

If people want something done, they call me. As long as it's not illegal, as long as it doesn't make my skin crawl, whatever it is—I'll fix it.

They need an event thrown together with no notice? I'll do it.

They need the press talking about something? Easy enough.

They need to protect an old building, to secure permission for a film shoot, to negotiate a stalled deal?

I'm the end of the road. I'm the person you call when all your other options are tapped out. And I charge top dollar for the privilege.

Except when it's Jake calling, of course. Then I cover costs, and that's it. Because for Jake, I'd do anything, and for his baby sister—I can't let myself think it. Thoughts are dangerously close to actions.

"Roxy," I murmur. Unlike earlier, I know she's in there. I

can hear the creak of her bed springs and the rustle of her blankets. "Roxy. Can we speak for a moment?"

"No." Her voice is muffled. Like she's speaking into a pillow. I check my watch, but it's not yet midnight. Whenever I've stayed at her and Jake's apartment before, she's always been a night owl. I'm not waking her up.

I rap again, quietly. Jake may be sleeping, but he's only a few feet away down the corridor. I don't want to tempt fate more than I already am.

"Just for a second, sweetheart. Then I'll leave you be."

She huffs so loud, I hear it through the door. I just have time to wipe the smile from my face before she wrenches the door open, scowling up at me with her hair mussed. She's wearing thick, patterned leggings, hiking socks and one of Jake's old college sweatshirts. There are tiny pink crease lines on her cheek from the pillow, and her mouth is pressed in a firm line.

She's perfect. So damn beautiful. My heart squeezes painfully in my chest, and I almost reach for her before I snatch my hand back.

That's not why I'm here. I'm setting things right. Then I'm going to put some much-needed space between us.

"About earlier—" I begin, but she holds up a palm.

"Forget it." Her voice is gravelly. Is that from tiredness? Or is she getting a cold? Or—worst of all—did I actually make her cry? "It doesn't matter. I'll get dressed in the bathroom next time. Okay? Now please leave me alone."

She turns away, already shutting the door, and I panic, blocking it with a palm. She looks up at me, startled, and I watch the pulse hammering in her throat.

Is she scared of me? Or excited?

"Wait. Yes, that's fine, but I want to apologize too. I'm sorry for saying those things, Roxy."

"What things?" She raises her chin. Yeah, she's not scared of me anymore. "The part about how I was trying to tempt the crew? Or the part about my 'perfect body'?"

She's got me. I swallow hard, eyes darting down the corridor to Jake's door.

"All of it," I rasp. "Forgive me."

I can't keep the misery and self loathing from my voice, and that more than anything seems to soften her. Roxy's shoulders relax, and she scans me again with fresh eyes.

"Are you okay?" she whispers. Shy again.

"I will be once you've forgiven me."

Her mouth quirks up. A pink flush creeps over her cheeks, and I'd give anything to trace it with my fingertips. With my *teeth.*

"I forgive you." Those quiet words flood through me, soothing and cool. Then her nose wrinkles. "But don't be mean again."

"I won't," I promise. Just the fact that I've hurt her at all, even in a small way—it hollows out my insides. I'll do *anything* to avoid that a second time. I want to go back to the way she looked at me before. With hero worship in her wide eyes.

"Where's Jake?" she asks, chewing on her lip and looking past me.

"Asleep." I don't mention the whisky. The second shameful thing I've done today. She nods, relieved, and smiles shyly as she steps back into her cabin.

"Goodnight, Damian."

My reply is hoarse. "Goodnight."

Her door shuts before I'm ready. I wasn't done looking at her, damn it. I didn't manage to get a whiff of her scent. Roxy changes her shampoo more often than other people change their shirts, and it's become a shameful obsession of mine to try and guess each new scent.

I can't sneak through her bag to see if I've guessed right until I can smell her better. Until I find an excuse to hug her, pressing my nose to the crown of her head.

I pinch the bridge of my nose, letting myself into my own cabin.

I am the worst kind of man.

Roxy

There's something different about Damian. Over the last week of the trip, he's been... distracted. On edge.

Usually, he's the ice man—cool and collected. Completely impossible to throw off his game. But over the last seven days at sea, he's become rougher. Wilder. His moods are more extreme, and quicker to change. He never takes them out on anyone, but you can *see* it if you're looking.

I'm always looking.

It starts with my sketchpad. With a charcoal hovering over the blank page as I stare out glassy-eyed at the waves. I've already done scores of ocean sketches, I've cataloged every inch of the boat, and I need something new. A fresh inspiration.

Damian strides past, talking in low tones with the captain. The two men have taken well to each other, each recognizing a calm authority in the other without feeling the need to scrap for dominance. I catch Jake watching them sometimes, a funny look in his eye.

My poor big brother is jealous. Now he knows how *I* feel.

Damian Flint is a hot commodity. Everyone wants a piece of this man. And I want several pieces, all of them in fact, but the only way I can possess them is on paper.

That's why I do it. Sketch him that first time. It's scrawled and messy, a warm up sketch to loosen my wrist and get into the rhythm, but it flows through me as naturally as the sea water pounding the hull. My hand was *made* to sketch Damian. I know every line of his body; every plane of his face. All his seasons and moods.

Once I've started, it's impossible to stop.

In my defense, I do try. I sketch Jake and the captain and the other crew members too. None of them inspire me like Damian. So I retreat into the pages of my sketchbook, hitching my knees up and tucking away into hidden alcoves, watching him and drawing. Capturing every glimpse of him that I can steal.

It's funny. I've come all the way out here hoping for inspiration, and I've found it in a man from home.

The sketches start innocent. They're realistic—just exactly what I can see, translated to the paper. Damian stood on deck, one hand resting on the railing, the other stroking his jaw as he stares at the horizon. Damian laughing with Jake. Conferring seriously with the captain. Playing cards with the crew below deck.

Damian walking past my open doorway in just his jeans, a towel slung around his neck.

Hypocrite. I pressed extra hard against the paper as I drew that sketch.

If he notices me watching him, he shows no sign. And he never asks to see what I'm doing. None of them do—which is fine, obviously. They're all here to do a job; I'm the lucky one getting the free trip. But it makes me cocky. Daring. My drawings get bolder, wilder, just like Damian's polish is wearing off the longer we're at sea.

That first sketch without a shirt is a turning point. I know what his body looks like now beneath his clothes. The top half of it at least, and when the top half is that broad and toned and substantial, there's no way the bottom half would be a let down.

Not with the way his jeans cling to his muscled thighs. I swallow hard, wiping my sleeve over my forehead.

I'm tucked away on deck, out of sight and out of mind, scribbling away in my sketchpad. For some of the drawings, I take infinite care, agonizing over every tiny line; every patch of shading. For others, I loosen my wrist and rush myself, trying to capture him in quick, broad strokes.

Those are the ones that suit him most, in the end. The urgent, untethered sketches.

This one is like that. A free drawing, with little care but lots of feeling. I begin to draw Damian as I can see him—leaning against the deck railing, mouth twisted as he scans something on his phone—but my hand quickly takes over. Has a better idea.

Damian shirtless again. Yes. After all, why cover him up when I've seen how godlike he is beneath those layers? With the wind still tugging his hair, but his eyes raised. Narrowed. Staring straight out at me through the page.

I bite my lip, shading the hollow of his throat. If he'd only look at me like that—well. I might not survive it.

I flip the page as soon as I'm done, eager now. I've drawn him standing—now I lay him out on the cot in my cabin, pillowing his arm beneath his head. I've seen the bulge of those biceps, felt the swell of them during our rare hugs.

I add a cocky smile. I've never seen *that*.

Not filled with dark promise. Sensual and primal, seductive enough to make my thighs tremble.

I'm getting worked up by my own sketch. *Jeez*. Is this what sea-madness is?

I flip the page again, cheeks hot, and keep going regardless. This time, I draw something even worse. I draw us *together*. Sketch after sketch of our bodies entwined. Me on my knees in front of him, his big hands twisted in my hair. Him taking me up against a wall, my arms looped around his neck and his hands gripping my ass tight enough to bruise. Him behind me while I brace myself on all fours, his top lip curled back in a snarl as he works out all that pent up frustration.

So many sketches. So many I lose count. I draw and draw until the sun slips toward the horizon and I'm left alone on the deck. My hand cramps and I shake it out, hissing between my teeth, before diving back in. I'm fevered. I'm a woman possessed.

"Roxy?" My heart slams against my rib cage. I let out a yelp, almost dropping my sketchbook. Damian frowns at me, concerned, his hands in his pockets. His eyes drift down towards my sketchpad—

I slam it shut.

"What's up?" I sound off to my own ears. Strangled and high pitched.

"It's time to eat. What's going on?"

He means my sketchpad. My scarlet cheeks and shifting eyes. I shake my head desperately, too tongue-tied to speak.

"May I see that?" he asks quietly.

161

"No," I say, the word escaping on a gasp. His frown deepens. "Why not?"

"I... I..."

"There's no reason to be embarrassed. I already know how talented you are." His praise trickles through me, sparkling and warm, but I don't have time to appreciate it. I need to change the subject right now.

"It's not ready," I blurt. "I'll show you when it's done. Okay?" He nods slowly, his expression doubtful. I toss the sketchpad to one side, pushing to my feet and bouncing on my toes. The bright smile plastered over my face makes my cheeks ache.

"Let's look for wildlife. While the light is still good." I grab his hand, even though we don't do this. We don't touch each other. But to my surprise, he doesn't pull away. If anything, Damian squeezes me back, gentle but encouraging. And he lets me drag him to the railing, staring out at the waves.

Now and then, over the last week, pods of dolphins and the occasional whale have come to visit the boat. I peer out desperately for something now—the glimpse of a fin, a seal's head—but there's nothing. Just the choppy waves, gilded silver by the setting sun.

"I don't think they're coming." He lowers his head, murmuring against my temple. My breath catches, butterflies swirling in my chest. "They must know it's dinner time."

I gasp out a laugh. He straightens up, pleased, and lets go of my hand.

The absence of his touch makes me ache.

But then his arm wraps around my shoulder, warm and heavy, and he steers me back below deck. I go in a daze, tripping over my own feet as I try to catalog every sensation. Commit his touch and scent to memory.

Roxy

I don't remember until hours later and I'm back in my cabin—I left the sketchbook on deck.

Damian

There's something wrong with Roxy.

Or not *wrong* exactly, but... off. I know this girl. I've known her for years—since Jake and I were teenagers and she was a tiny baby. I've watched her grow into a young woman and a talented artist. She's funny and quick-witted and shy.

And now she's nervous. Her teeth are practically chattering with extra energy; she darts glances around like a prey animal. She's been hiding herself away from everyone on board, scribbling away in her sketchpad, a tiny frown creasing her forehead.

And she stares so intently at whatever she's drawing, that I *know* it's something significant. Something that's making her afraid.

I just want to make sure she's okay. That there's nothing sinister going on. I'm not going to-to *overstep*.

I'm checking in on her. Taking care of her. And that sketchpad is the way to do it. So when Roxy leaves it behind when we go below deck for dinner, I'm going to hell for

164

it, but I don't say anything. She said she'll show me when it's finished, but what if she's in danger? Or some kind of emotional turmoil?

I'm the fixer. Roxy is *mine.* And whatever the problem is, I'm going to fix it for her.

Dinner lasts an eternity. The whole meal I'm on edge, braced for Roxy to leap to her feet, remembering her sketchpad. But she doesn't—she eats quietly, stealing rare glances at me, and each time her gaze falls on me, my heart slams in my chest. At one point, she takes a bite of something and hums appreciatively.

I grip the edge of the table, my knuckles turning white.

When she heads back to her cabin, bidding everyone good-night, I can hardly believe my luck. I lunge up the stairs to the deck as soon as everyone else is distracted, striding to the spot where I found her sketching earlier.

It's still here. The pages are bloated and crackling, puffed up by use. And the black cover is spotted with drops of sea water, a lump of charcoal abandoned at its side.

"Roxy," I murmur, plucking up the sketchpad. "Forgive me, sweetheart." I flip it open, scanning her drawings by the light of the moon. The deck lurches beneath me, waves battering the hull, and I shift my feet wider to balance as I flick through the pages.

Seabirds.

Parts of the ship, rendered in stark light and shadows.

Roxy's messy cabin—I smile at the twisted bed covers.

Waves. Lots of waves.

I page through the book, frustration mounting. Surely, if this was all she'd been drawing, she'd have nothing to hide. Nothing to flush bright red and hide her sketchpad over. I flick faster and faster through the stiff pages, cursing under my breath, and I almost miss it—the drawing of me.

I'm standing by the railing. A breeze tugs at my hair, and a frown creases my forehead as I gaze out to sea. I stare down at the drawing, pulse thrumming louder and louder until it pounds in my ears.

She draws me?

I turn the page. My heart sinks.

It's a sketch of the captain.

"Fuck," I mutter, paging quicker again. I'm there a lot, but then so are the others. Jake most of all, then the captain, then a few of each of the crew. She's been drawing all of us, and if she draws me the most—well, I'm always around. I'm a convenient subject.

That's all it is, I tell myself sternly. *Don't get carried away.*

It would truly be the mark of a desperate man to read into this. To pretend that some drawings seem more wistful than others.

I turn another page and freeze.

Roxy has drawn me shirtless. Bare-chested, and when did she see me like that? She's captured every detail, down to the scar on my hip. Whenever it was, she studied me carefully. I scrub a hand down my face, willing my heartbeat to slow.

I'm staring out of the page. Eyes narrowed and fixed on the audience. Is that how she sees me? Angry and stern? I swallow hard, turning the page again.

It's me again. Stretched out on the bed in her cabin. This time I'm smiling, but there's a menace to it. Dark promise. I curse quietly, turning the page.

They're all of me. From this point forward, Roxy has only drawn me. And they go a simple shirtless sketch—reasonably innocent, no different from any life study—to pictures of the two of us together.

Roxy on her knees in front of me, her small hands resting on my thighs. Roxy grinding into my lap; on hands and knees; dwarfed beneath my body. She's drawn us in every position she could think of, and when I remember how flushed her cheeks were, how bright her eyes—

"Fuck." I snap the sketchpad closed.

I shouldn't have looked. That—that was wrong. I shouldn't have seen any of this. It's private, and what's more, I *know* Roxy. I know how crushed she'd be if she knew I'd seen these.

I place the sketchpad back exactly where I found it. Dig my fists into my eyes and suck in a long, slow breath. I'll go back below deck. I can do this. I can be around her and not let slip what I've seen.

"Fucking hell," I mutter one last time, then turn to leave the deck.

Roxy stands a few feet behind me, eyes wide and face chalky white. Her gaze darts between me and the book behind me, her lower lip wobbling, and god, I want to slam my head on the deck as I watch her heart breaking.

"You promised..." she trails off, shaking her head like she can't believe it. Like she can't believe this is happening. "You said you wouldn't look."

"Roxy." I reach out a hand but she's gone, whipping around and scurrying back below deck. I sigh and scoop up the sketchpad again, tucking it under my arm. Better that Jake doesn't see this.

I give her a few minutes. A chance to get back to her cabin before I follow. And in that time, I peer up at the stars. They wink down at me, ancient and knowing, and when I draw in each breath, the salt air burns my lungs.

I've hurt her. I've fucked up. Seeing that betrayal on her face—my chest tightens like a vice.

But even so, my traitorous cock pulses in my jeans, and those sketches flit through my brain. Our charcoal bodies, tangled up and gasping. Roxy's secret plea to the paper.

If she still wants me, I'll fix this for her too.

Her brother never needs to know.

Roxy

This can't be real. This can't be real.

This is a nightmare. Right?

There's no way that I really did something so stupid. Drew *sex* drawings of my brother's best friend, then left them laying out on deck where anyone could find them.

It's too stupid to believe, and the worst thing is… I don't think it *was* an accident. Not really.

I think I wanted Damian to see them. I think I wanted to plant that seed in his mind—the idea of the two of us together, naked and grasping.

I wanted to see his reaction. Well, I got it. *"Fucking hell."*

So humiliating. And I've truly played myself, because it's not like I can go away somewhere to lick my wounds. I'm stuck here for a whole week still, on this boat with him, his broad shoulders and firm jaw and smoldering brown eyes everywhere I look.

I groan and bury my face in the pillow. Seriously, *what was I thinking?*

"Roxy." Normally I love to hear his voice. The low, rich timber of it. And him saying my name? Forget it. But right this moment, I'd rather leap out of the porthole than see Damian.

"Go away," I yell into the pillow.

There's a sharp exhale. Halfway between a huff and a laugh. Then he's trying the handle, nudging at my door.

"It's locked," I grumble, just loud enough for him to hear. "Good to know you don't respect *any* boundaries, though."

There's a long silence. Then a sigh. The floor in the corridor creaks as he shifts his weight, his voice coming clearer through the door.

"You're right. I'm sorry I looked. I shouldn't have done that." I shake my head into the pillow, even though he can't see me. He's *sorry*? Oh, that's nice. I guess I won't be viscerally humiliated any more. "But, Roxy—" he lowers his voice. I have to strain to hear him. "I'm not sorry about what I saw."

Heat prickles over my skin, from my head to my toes. What does *that* mean? My mind races as I sit up in bed, staring at the locked cabin door as I gnaw on my lip.

He's not sorry about what he saw?

"Did you…" I clear my throat and speak a little louder. "Did you… like them?"

"*Yes.*" His reply is immediate. He tries the handle again. "Let me in and I'll show you."

Oh my god. Oh my god, oh my god. My older brother is right down the hall. It's not even late yet, no one is asleep, and Damian wants to come in? To be alone in my bedroom? I swing my feet off the bed, standing and swaying in my chunky socks. The floor tilts beneath me as I stumble to the door and pause.

"Come on, sweetheart." He says it so quiet, I don't know if

I'm even meant to hear. I hold my breath and spin the lock.

The door pushes open straight away, Damian's bulk crowding through the doorway, then he slams it shut and turns the lock behind him. He seems even bigger than before, vibrating with energy, and when he turns to face me, his eyes are hard.

He pushes my sketchpad into my hands.

"Better keep that safe," he rasps. "You don't want anyone to see."

That's not quite true. I scratch my nail over the cover, then go for broke.

"Actually, I wanted *you* to see."

His chest expands. Damian stares down at me, every line of him rigid and terse. If I didn't know him as well as I do, I'd think he was angry.

He's not angry. He's about to snap.

"What are you going to show me?" He needs that final push. Damian is a good man, and loyal to my brother. He may have come here, but I can see the conflict warring in his eyes. I take a deep breath and place my hand on his chest.

That's all. Just that simple touch. I've probably touched him there dozens of times before. But this time, it's different. This time, we're crammed inside my cabin, locked in together beside my messy bed, and the sketchpad gripping in my other hand is full of things I can't take back.

I can't, and I don't want to, not when Damian grunts and grabs me by the ass, lifting me up to wrap my legs around his waist. The sketchpad falls to the bed, forgotten. I loop my arms around his neck, gasping as his hard, trapped length prods the seam of my leggings.

"You're trying to push me," he says hoarsely, rutting against me as he speaks. I whimper, burying my face in his throat.

"You want to see how far I'll go, sweetheart?"

I nod, the delicious friction of him rubbing against me tying my tongue in knots. "Yes," I gasp when his hand cracks against my ass. "I want all of it."

He curses darkly, and it's just like up on deck. When he flicked through my drawings of him and swore. But then, I thought he was disgusted. Annoyed.

Now I know better. He wants me just as badly.

"I'll fix this for you," he's muttering. "Are you aching, sweetheart? I can make that go away." I nod and rub against him, rolling my hips, rubbing my face in his throat like I can coat myself in his scent. "Jake never needs to know," he says quietly, and I pause, heart sinking.

He doesn't?

So this is... a one-time thing?

A crack splinters down the center of my chest. I keep my face hidden, eyes screwed shut in pain, but I won't show him this part of me. *These* feelings are even more private than my sketchpad. And when I've finally caught my breath, hips starting to roll again, I'm determined.

If one time is all I get, I'll make the most of it. I'll soak up every atom of Damian Flint that he'll give me, and when he leaves my cabin... I'll let him go. Try to move on.

Still, when his mouth crashes onto mine, kissing me hard and fast and desperate—my heart aches so badly it brings tears to my eyes.

"What's this?" Damian leans back, capturing a stray tear with his thumb. "Have I hurt you? Do you want to stop?"

"No." I fist my hands in his shirt, and force the words out. Force myself to be brave. "I want to keep going. I want..." I grit my teeth and meet his eyes. "I want your cock."

Something ripples through him. His eyes darken. His hands squeeze tighter on my ass.

"Roxy," he chokes out. "I shouldn't..."

I rake my teeth up his throat. "You definitely should."

That's all it takes. He spins us around, lowering to sit on my bed. I scramble back off his lap, tugging my leggings and panties down, and the noise he makes as I drop them makes my head spin. I go to climb back on his thighs but he moves even faster, sliding down to lay length-ways and patting his chest.

"Up here, sweet girl."

I frown, doing as he says. "You want me to sit up here?"

"Close." He smirks. "On my face."

Oh.

I've—I've heard of this. But I've never done it, never done *any* of it. Before today, I'd never even kissed a man. How could I, when my heart only ached for my brother's best friend?

"I don't know what I'm doing," I whisper. I expect him to sigh, but heat flares in his eyes. He scoops my ass into his hands again and lifts me forward. He lines me up, settling my knees on either side of his head, and when he urges me to lower myself down, I jump at the sudden contact.

His chin is scratchy. Rough with his evening shadow. And bony against my soft flesh. But then there's the warmth of his breath, and he opens his mouth, and his tongue—

Oh. I scrabble at the wall, head tipping back on my shoulders.

Damian licks at me with broad strokes, delving and exploring, and when he suckles on my clit, my thighs start to twitch. He groans as he licks me, like I'm the best thing he's ever tasted, his hands squeezing and releasing my ass.

God.

I rock against him, shyly at first, then braver and bolder the longer we go.

"That's it," he grinds out into my pussy. "Take what you want, sweet girl."

I rock harder, faster, and when his tongue plunges inside me, I shudder and quake, falling apart at the seams. A hoarse cry passes my lips, and I duck my chin, shaking as wave after wave passes through me.

Holy shit. I slump, remembering at the last second to scoot back and sit on Damian's chest. He watches me carefully, chin slick, stroking his palms up and down my thighs.

"Did you like that, Roxy?"

I nod dazedly. I can't speak.

"Do you still want—" A knock at the door makes us both freeze. We stare at each other in horror as Jake's voice floats through the door.

"Rox? Are you in there?" The door handle jiggles. Does *no one* on this boat respect a closed door? "You seemed kind of weird at dinner. You want to come out and play cards?"

I sit on the sculpted chest of my brother's best friend, breath wheezing in and out of my lungs. There's no way to make this look good. I'm-I'm *naked* from the waist down, and I lurch off the bed with wobbly legs. I fumble my leggings back on with shaking fingers as Damian pushes upright, making the bed quickly and wiping his face. Then he sits back down and puts his face in his hands.

Okay. Okay. I scan desperately for my panties but they're gone.

Okay. This is happening.

"Hi!" I spin the lock and yank the door open. "Um, sorry. I

174

wanted to talk to Damian about something."

Jake stands in the corridor, peering over my shoulder. His gaze bounces between my flushed cheeks and Damian's stony expression. His eyes narrow.

"What's going on?" He directs the question to me. It's quiet. Commanding. Sometimes Jake forgets that I'm grown now. That he's not my stand-in parent any more.

"I just told you," I say, breathless. "I needed to ask Damian a favor—"

"What kind of favor?" His question is low. Deadly. The look he shoots Damian over my shoulder—it's like he doesn't recognize his own best friend.

"Um." My cheeks flare bright red. "I wanted to ask him about boys."

"About—" Jake cuts himself off, shaking his head. "What? *Why?* Why wouldn't you come to me?"

"To her older brother?" Damian asks wryly, pushing to his feet. I glance back at him, but he won't meet my eye. "Give her a break, man. No one wants to talk to their sibling about this stuff."

"Right. Yeah." Jake brightens, all that suspicion gone. It's as if it never happened. "I hope you told her none of them are good enough for her."

"Shut up," I mumble, half touched, half horrified.

"Roxy knows." Damian squeezes past me, and he *ruffles my hair.* I blink at his shoulder blades passing through the doorway, stunned.

"So you wanna play cards?" Jake asks again, grinning at me. "I'll let you win a few rounds."

"In your dreams," I murmur. Damian casts one last look at me, his face unreadable, then strides away down the corridor.

The thud of his boots echoes back to me, each one clanging through my brain.

...That's it. That's *it?* He does *that* to me, then just walks away without another word? Ruffles my hair like some kid and strolls away? My jaw snaps shut, grinding my teeth, and I barely manage to wave Jake off, claiming a headache.

I don't want to play cards. I don't want to see anyone.

I'm sick of these men.

Damian

I thought I could handle this. That I could ease Roxy's ache, then do the right thing. Put some space between us. After all, this is just a crush—hell, if we weren't literally at sea, she wouldn't look twice at me. She'd want someone her own age.

That doesn't make it any easier. Every morning that she avoids my eye at breakfast, every time I glance over at her on the deck and she looks tired and pale, my resolve crumbles a little more.

It's the right thing to do.

The right thing to do.

So why does it feel like I'm fucking this up? Like I'm hurting this sweet girl, turning her pale and sad and cold? Like I've crushed her hopes.

But that's bullshit. Maybe she hoped for more of an encounter. More of a fling. Well, as tempting as that sounds—and my body is *constantly* ready for hers now—my heart couldn't take it. Maybe it seems weak, but I don't care.

If I let her, she'd crack me open down the middle.

Play around behind her brother's back for the thrill. Mess around with an older, more experienced man. Then go back to her life, to the art schools she's been secretly applying for. To guys her own age.

I wouldn't survive it.

So this is the right thing to do. I'm protecting her from the worst of me—all the dark and desperate things I want to do to her. And I'm guarding myself too, sparing myself the pain that she doesn't even realize she'd inflict on me. Roxy has owned my heart and body and soul since she became a woman.

I should never have let it get this far.

It's the last night of the trip before she speaks to me again. Not by choice, no matter how many times I've tried to catch her eye. No—I corner her in the galley kitchen, helping out with the dishes. She's elbow-deep in suds, scrubbing at dirty plates, and bastard that I am, I take my chance.

"Roxy."

Her shoulders tense. Standing behind her, I can safely admire the slope of her neck. Her glossy dark hair, scraped back into a high ponytail.

Hair like that gives a man ideas. Thoughts of running his fingers through those tresses; of the strands brushing over his bare stomach; of wrapping that ponytail around his hand and pulling her head back to bare her throat.

"Yes?" she asks carefully. "Did I miss a plate?"

I glance around the kitchen, at the crew member mopping the floor, before leaning in to murmur in her ear.

"You can't avoid me forever."

"Sure I can."

My chest tightens. *"Please.* I just want to talk. So things are okay between us back on land. You're..." I swallow. "You're

178

very important to me, Roxy." Understatement of the century. "I need you in my life."

She sucks in a sharp breath, scrubbing so hard at the plates that flecks of dish soap fly through the air.

"Is that right?" *Scrub, scrub, scrub.* "Because it didn't seem like that the other night. It *seemed,*" she slams the clean plate on the drying rack and reaches for a knife. I reach around and pass her a bowl quickly. "It *seemed* like you got what you wanted and left."

"You think I used you," I say flatly.

"And you think I'm a child." She slams the bowl onto the rack and spins around. We're close, chest to chest, and her eyes flash up at me. She smacks my shirt, leaving a damp hand print. "I'm not a kid anymore. I can make my own decisions. And I know when someone's being a jerk."

"You're right. I'm sorry." I don't know what I'm doing. What my plan was, coming here. All I know is that hurt is swirling in those gorgeous eyes, and I'm the one who put it there. I cradle her face, rubbing my thumb over her cheekbone, and Roxy lets out a ragged sigh. Her eyes drift shut.

Remembering too late, I glance over my shoulder. The crew member is gone, the mop abandoned on the floor.

"Roxy," I growl, my heart lunging against my rib cage. "Do you think I don't want you?"

She bites her lip, not answering.

That's answer enough.

I lunge down, capturing her mouth with mine. Fuck doing the right thing. Fuck protecting my heart. My sweet girl is hurting, and I could no more deny her right now than I could cut off my own arm. I kiss her with every ounce of the longing I've felt. With all the pent-up frustration I've been carrying around over the last six months.

Every time I came over to their apartment to see Jake, and Roxy strutted past in tiny pajama shorts.

Every time she hugged me, her soft body pressing against mine.

Every time she laughed her throaty laugh.

And those sketches. Those fucking sketches.

I show Roxy what it's like to kiss a *man.* One who knows her, body and soul, and is about to make her weep from pleasure. And she moans into my mouth, kissing me back just as fiercely, her body bowing towards me and rubbing against my swollen cock.

"We should go to my cabin," she gasps between kisses. "Someone will see."

"I don't care." I grab her ass and set her down on the counter. She's in the same leggings as last time—just another way she's been torturing me—and her ankles lock behind my waist automatically. We're not touching, not yet, but I can feel the damp heat of her pussy, scorching me even from here.

"Roxy." I take her by the chin. "This isn't a fling. Do you understand?" I rock against her as I talk, dragging the hard length of my cock, encased in jeans, up and down her core. "If you let me inside this pussy, you're mine. There's no going back. I don't care what Jake or any other fucker says. You're *mine.*"

It's too much. I'm letting the mask slip too far, showing just how primal my feelings are for her. But Roxy nods up at me, glassy eyed, and catches my wrist in her hand. She drags my thumb to her lips.

"I understand." She sucks me inside.

God. The searing heat of her mouth, her swirling tongue,

those wide eyes fixed on mine as her cheeks hollow—I groan, thrusting my hips harder against her. In an ideal world, I'd have planned this moment. Planned the kind of first time she deserves. But she's nipping against the pad of my thumb, thrusting her hips against me in turn, and it's too fucking late.

I need in there *now*.

"Sweetheart," I rasp, yanking at her leggings with my free hand. "Fuck. Get those down." She lifts her hips, wriggling those leggings to her knees, then hitches her legs up and tugs her panties to the side. I pause, chest heaving as I stare at her pussy. Pink and swollen and slick.

Am I really going to do this to her? Take her like an animal on this counter, out in the kitchen where anyone could see?

"Stop it." She tugs at my shirt. "Whatever you're thinking, stop it. I want this."

I stare hypnotized at her slit. "But—"

"No buts." She tugs my pants open, drawing out my cock in her palm. She squeezes once, drawing her fist along my length. I hiss, bucking into her hand, and she fixes me with a look. "Or do you want me to beg?"

Yes, god, yes, I want that, but not this time. This time, if she pleads for my cock, I'll blow where I stand. I crowd closer, lining up with her entrance, then hold her gaze as I ease the first inch inside.

Her wince breaks my heart. Smashes it into a thousand pieces, leaving only jagged edges and dust in my chest.

"Does it hurt?" I rasp, pulling back. She locks her ankles and tugs me closer, impaling herself another inch.

"Yes," she breathes, rolling her hips slightly. She wets her bottom lip. "But it's a good kind of hurt."

And *fuck*, we don't have time to unpack all that, but there will be time—weeks, months, years. A lifetime of this beautiful girl and this perfect pussy, and I let out another groan as I sink deeper inside. She's tight and hot, as wet as her mouth, and that eases the way. Lets me push closer, closer. And though Roxy clings to me, arms shaking, her head tipped back, I can feel her pussy twitching. Can feel it clamp down on me, sucking me further inside.

"You like this cock?" I nip her ear. She nods, whimpering.

"Uh-huh. I want it so bad."

"You're getting it." I slam the rest of the way home, cursing under my breath at the perfect clasp of her. Her legs are twitching on either side of my waist, and I run soothing palms up and down her thighs. "There, sweet girl. I'm all the way in."

"It's so big." She buries her face against my throat. "I can feel you *everywhere.*"

She can't say that shit to me. Not without sawing through the last of my control. I snarl, snapping my hips forward, jerking her back against the counter and sending a container of wooden spoons clattering over. I grip her ass cheeks in both hands, grip bruising, dragging her closer to the edge, and *roll* into her. Over and over, tortuously slow, until we're both gasping for the same air.

She's everything. Every part as good as I'd dreamed.

She's oblivion.

And she's mine. Mine. *Mine.*

"You feel that?" I tilt my hips, dragging my length over her g-spot. Roxy cries out, twitching in my arms. "That's the only cock you're ever going to need. It's all fucking yours, baby."

She's whispering something under her breath, and it sounds a lot like *ohmygodohmygodohmygod.* I reach between us and rub her clit, pinching and rolling it between my fingers, and she *squeaks.*

Fuck. I need to hear that sound again. I need to hear it every day for the rest of my life. I need it for my goddamn text alert. I lick a stripe up her neck, dragging my teeth over her pulse point, and I feel the exact moment that she comes.

Her breath hitches. Her muscles go rigid. And her pussy clamps down so hard on my cock, I see stars. I keep thrusting into her, rubbing her clit and working her through it, wringing every last drop of pleasure out of her. I grit my teeth, concentrating harder than I ever have in my goddamn life. And only when Roxy slumps in my arms, her strings cut, do I bury myself to hilt and finally let go.

"*Fuck.* Sweetheart." I drop my forehead onto her shoulder and empty inside her, filling her to the brim. She gasps at the sudden wet warmth, urging me closer with her heels. Dirty girl.

"Damian." Her voice is quiet. Dazed but something else. I look up.

She's… unsure. Her fingertips trail along my jaw, and she swallows hard before she finally meets my eyes. Whatever she sees there, burning in my gaze, chases those final fears away.

A smile breaks over her face, cheeks dimpling, and I chuckle as she leans forward and nips my bottom lip. I wrap her tight in my arms, cradling her to my chest, still hard and pulsing inside her.

"What the fuck is this?"

We freeze. Roxy lets out a sound—a soft, horrified cry—and I pivot us slightly. Shielding her from view.

"Give us a moment." My tone brooks no argument. I'm not asking Jake; I'm telling him. The pain and fury was clear in his voice, but I won't have Roxy shamed or made to feel small.

"Are you fucking kidding me?"

"Out!" I roar, turning and pinning him with my glare. Jake flinches in the kitchen doorway, his face already pinched with rage, and starts forward.

"Jake." Her voice is so small, muffled by my shirt. My heart twists. "Please. Don't."

He stops. Sucks in a long, shuddering breath, staring at the two of us like he doesn't even know us.

Then my best friend turns on his heel and storms out of the kitchen.

Roxy

"I can't believe this." I bury my face in my hands, spinning in slow circles in the kitchen. We're dressed again, but there's no way I'm going out there. I'm not facing my older brother after he just caught me having sex—caught me *losing my virginity*—on a counter.

I live in this kitchen now. I hope it will be a good life. Maybe I'll finally learn to bake.

Damian says nothing, wiping down the counter with a horribly blank face. He shut down the second Jake walked away, cleaning us up and setting me down on the floor without a single word.

Every minute that passes without his reassurance—I die a little inside.

"Damian?" I whisper finally, wrapping my arms around my waist and squeezing tight. He stills, bent over the counter. "I'm..." My voice breaks. I try again. "I'm so sorry."

"What?" He wheels around, eyes sparking with fury. I cringe backwards, almost tripping over the mop, but when Damian

185

lunges forward, catching my shoulders, his grip is gentle. Always so gentle. "What on earth do you have to be sorry for?" He gives me a little shake. Makes me meet his eyes.

There are little flecks of gold in the brown. I'll have to draw him in color next time.

I gesture weakly at the doorway. "For screwing things up for you with Jake. For-for pushing you when I knew it meant trouble."

Damian stares at me for what feels like an age. Then he drops his forehead to mine, letting out a pained sigh.

"Roxy. Sweetheart. I don't regret a moment of it. And even if I did, you wouldn't be to blame."

"But—"

"There were two of us involved, correct?" I nod slowly, and his mouth quirks. "Then if there is blame, we'll share it."

Share it. Okay.

"Besides." Damian scrubs the back of his neck ruefully. "You warned me we'd get caught. I didn't care."

I bite my lip. "And you're the responsible one."

He snorts. "Guess we're all in trouble." We stand in a long silence, and the amusement drains from his face. That eerie blank expression comes back, and I shake him by the sleeve.

"What is it?"

He takes a second to notice my question. But when he does, he smiles down at me, strained but warm.

"Your brother is right to be angry."

"Because you're friends?"

He shrugs. "Partly. And because you're so young. Young and beautiful and funny and completely fucking irresistible." He buries his face in his hands as he speaks, finishing on a long groan, and I stifle a smile. I shuffle forward, wrapping my arms around him, resting my head on his forearms.

"He'll forgive us."

"He'll forgive *you*," Damian mutters.

"No." I press a kiss to each of his wrists. "We're a package deal. He'll forgive *us*."

* * *

Okay, so I kind of exaggerated how confident I feel to Damian. The truth is, when I walk down the corridor to our cabins, I feel like I'm walking to the gallows. And when I knock on Jake's door, my heart is lodged somewhere at the back of my throat.

There's no answer. Silence. I turn on my heel, chewing on my lip as I decide where to look first.

He's not in my cabin. Not in Damian's, sharpening a knife. And he's not in any of the common spaces below deck. Damian grabs my elbow as I walk past him to the stairs, finally emerging from the kitchen.

"Good luck." He kisses my forehead. "He loves you. It'll be okay."

I nod, too tongue-tied to speak suddenly, and climb the steps to the upper deck. It's inky dark, no lights except for a few of the boat's dim bulbs and the moon shining overhead. The waves rolling all around are glossy black, given an oily sheen by the moonlight. The air that slaps my cheeks is icy cold, stinging with salt, and I breathe it in gratefully.

I find Jake by the railings. He leans on his elbows, a dark shadow against the blanket of stars. He must hear me approach, but he doesn't turn around. Doesn't acknowledge me at all.

My stomach swoops queasily. Jake—Jake is all the real family I have.

Part of me wants to beg. To drop to my knees and plead for his forgiveness, giving excuses for what I've done. But if I do that—if that apologize for loving Damian—I'll make what we have together something shameful.

Still, I'm not entirely innocent. So I square my shoulders, raise my chin, and apologize for the one thing I *am* sorry for.

"I'm sorry you saw that."

Jake scoffs and says nothing. His shoulders are set with anger, and I can practically hear him vibrating from here. I lick my lips and keep going.

"We should have kept it to the cabins."

That gets him talking. He whirls around, a hand digging through his dark hair, his face pale in the moonlight.

"Are you f—are you kidding me, Roxy? That's all? You wish you'd screwed my best friend behind closed doors?"

I wince, but my voice is clear. "Yes. That's what I'm sorry for. The *only* part, Jake."

"You—I—" He splutters, my chatterbox brother shocked into silence for the first time in his life. I hold up a palm.

"I hope you can forgive us. I hope you can be happy for me." My voice cracks. "I love him, Jake. And he loves me. So…" I trail off and shrug. "That's all."

I turn to go, ready to drown myself in a hot shower. But Jake's voice stops me short. He sounds wrecked, but… rueful.

"Roxy. Wait." I do as he asks, trying not to tap my foot with impatience as the silence stretches on. I've just opened my mouth to tell him goodnight when he wraps me in his arms.

"Jake." I burrow into my big brother's arms, gasping big lungfuls of salty air now the band around my chest is loosening.

He rubs slow circles on my back, his nose pressed in my hair.

"You can do better," he mutters. I kick his shin and he barks a laugh. Then, more serious, he says: "If he hurts you, I'll kill him."

"I know." I squash closer, sighing. Jake sniffs my head, then coughs.

"Ew. I can smell him on you."

"Shut up!" I push him away, but he's laughing. And when I turn to go back below deck, he comes with me, shoulders a bit more relaxed. "Please don't torture Damian," I whisper as we duck back inside. "He loves you too."

Jake shrugs one shoulder, but he can't hide that he's pleased. "Maybe. No promises, Rox."

Damian

Five Years Later

I stroll up behind my wife where she's curled in her favorite armchair, a sketchpad balanced on her knees. Her lump of charcoal moves swiftly over the paper, drawing two plump faces, two tiny bodies, two pairs of grasping hands. I lean over Roxy's shoulder, smirking when she jumps, and hum at the half-done drawing of our twin sons.

"You scared me!" She blows out a breath and laughs, turning her face for a kiss. "The boys just went down."

I straighten, peering into the shared crib, so much burning emotion in my chest that it chokes me. Roxy is my world. And now these boys…

There is no luckier man on earth.

I nod at her sketch "Is that for your gallery show?"

She scoffs, brushing a speck of charcoal off the page. "No. This is garbage. It's for Jake."

"I'll try not to be offended."

Roxy squeals at her big brother's voice, launching out of her armchair and sending her sketchpad flying. I round the chair and pick it up, smoothing the pages flat as she hurls herself across the room for a hug.

Jake's a busy man. Everyone wants a piece of his talent. But the only people who get a piece of *him* are in this room.

Even me. It took a while, but we're finally back where we were. He just needed to see me treat Roxy right, like the angel that she is.

I don't blame him. He's right to demand the best for her.

"How long are you here? Will you stay for a few days? Where are you going next—" Roxy blasts him with questions, talking a mile a minute. She grabs his arms and drags him towards the crib, her voice dropping to a stage whisper as they near the babies.

"Jeez." He peers down at them, eyes wide. "They're cuter in real life than on paper."

"I know, right?" Roxy beams, unoffended. She's so proud of our sons. She showed them off to the delivery man yesterday. And suddenly, seeing her smile in the shaft of sunlight from the window, I'm eager to know when Jake will leave.

We scarred him for life once. We won't do it again. But god, my wife is fucking gorgeous.

True bliss is when I'm lodged deep inside her. When she urges me on with her heels at my back, her moans ringing out through the room. She catches me looking at her now, and she must read the thoughts right there on my face, because she smirks. Sultry and knowing. Jake bends over the cot, cooing and blissfully ignorant, so I let her see a glimpse of it.

The maddening force of my love. My *need* for her. I've only been gone for a few hours, and already I'm half-mad with craving.

Roxy shivers and bites her lip.

Yeah. Jake better not stay too long.

My wife and I have some catching up to do.

IV

Arctic Star

Description

I live in the wilderness by choice. I'm no good with people.

But when a terrified young woman knocks on my cabin door, I have no choice but to offer her shelter.

She's a puzzle. Lost and exhausted in the Arctic circle, with nothing but a ratty backpack and a torn winter coat.

And it takes me way too long to notice—she doesn't speak. She can't speak. My sweet little runaway is mute.

That's fine. She has no reason to fear me. And no reason to be ashamed.

We'll be outcasts together.

Because she's not leaving. It's not safe out there.

And she's mine.

Harlow

The ancient bus grinds to a halt, settling heavier onto its wheels with a hiss. My forehead rocks against the fogged up window and I jerk awake, blinking and trying to remember where on earth I am.

Outside the windows, snow capped mountains loom in the distance and great grassy plains sway with wildflowers. White cotton candy puffs of clouds float through azure skies, and large birds of prey ride the air currents high above.

No. Seriously.

Where am I?

I lurch to my feet, yanking my padded coat and beat-up old backpack from the luggage rack. It has everything I own inside it, and it's still not two-thirds full. I shoulder it and push between the seats, catching on both sides of the aisle. I scan as I walk, but there are no other passengers. Not out here.

Wherever *this* even is. Why the hell did I go and fall asleep anyway? Sure, I've been traveling non-stop for three days. Trying to put as many miles as I can between my uncle and I.

Marry me off to the creepy old neighbor? No way. Nope. Not happening. I got out of there faster than my aunt goes through vodka, and I'm not ever going back.

They think because I don't speak, I don't *think*. That I don't have opinions. Feelings.

Well, I *feel* that they're shitty excuses for family. So I'm out. Harlow Lane is gonna make her own way.

"End of the route." The craggy old bus driver nods at the bus sign standing lopsided by the side of the road. There's a dent in the pole, like it's been hit by a truck. Or out here, maybe a moose. He swivels in his seat, blinking watery eyes at me. Poor guy. He looks tired out too. "Unless you wanna buy a ticket back to town?"

Right. The town. The stop I was *aiming* for. Until I overshot by... well, however many miles.

Too late now. I already spent my last dollar. And I cried out all my tears for this shit-show way back on my first bus. So it looks like I'm getting off here.

The end of the route.

I shake my head and the driver shrugs.

"Suit yourself. Get on down, then."

I wave a thank you and hop down onto the tarmac. My joints are stiff from sitting upright for so many hours, and I roll my head on my neck as the bus pulls away. It does a lumbering three point turn right there in the road, then heads back the same way we came.

A bird chirrups. Something snuffles out in the shrubbery. I hitch my backpack higher on my shoulders and wrinkle my nose.

Town. Back down the road. Or... I spin in a circle and scan my surroundings. There are mountains. A distant treeline.

And nothing else but the tarmac scar of the road running through the landscape.

Either way might be quicker. Either might have shelter somewhere along the way, or even somewhere I could beg a job.

Just like either might have grizzly bears, or trigger-happy hunters, or even worse. A truck rumbles past as I ponder, slowing as it draws level with me. A handsome middle-aged man with chestnut hair peers out the window, one elbow resting on the ledge.

"You lost, sweetheart?"

I shake my head, fast. Always better to look confident. I know *that* much at least.

"You're a long way from town." He cocks his head, watching me. "You walking up to the lodge?"

The lodge. Sounds good. Sounds promising. Like a place with jobs, and food, and somewhere to sleep. More importantly, it sounds like a real reason I'd be on this road. Nothing to see here, mister.

I nod and smile, mustering all the fake confidence I can. The man grunts.

"Want a ride? Fine. Suit yourself." He pulls away fast, tires spinning. I watch him drive away down the tarmac, keeping my eyes glued on his truck until it disappears from view.

Why'd I have to fall asleep on that damn bus? Now I'm stuck out in the wilderness with strange men and the wide open skies.

I look back toward the town. On toward the lodge. Which is closer? No way of knowing.

If I had a coin left, I'd flip it. But I don't have much except the clothes on my back, so I take a deep breath and start walking.

Away from town, further into the wilderness. Further from my damn uncle and that crusty old neighbor.

I'll just go a little ways. Just enough to scope it out; to see if there are any jobs going up here. And if I don't find anything in the next hour or so, I'll turn back and hustle the way I came.

Maybe it's dumb. Maybe it's genius.

Only one way to find out.

* * *

I make it past the count of seven hundred before the bad feelings start. I can't explain it exactly; there are no sudden dark clouds gathering overhead, or mysterious rustlings in the brush off the tarmac. All I know is, one step I'm clicking my tongue and swinging my arms, day dreaming about a warm bed and a hot shower. And the next, the hairs stand straight up on the back of my neck, while a bead of icy cold sweat slides down my spine.

I don't believe in ghosts or anything. Bad luck or superstitions. Most of the bad stuff that's happened in my life, I can draw a direct line to the person that did it.

But I'm also not a total fool. I know that when my body's telling me something, it's time to put up and listen.

My boots scuff to a halt. I strain my eyes peering into every nook and cranny of the wild landscape—the tangle of shrubs and long grass and wildflowers on either side of the road, and in the distance, the tree line and the mountains. I make my eyes go all soft and blurry, the way hunters do, so I can pick out any flickers of movement.

Nothing. No predator creeping near. No grazing herd animals setting off my cave woman brain. I blow out a long breath, scanning, scanning.

The hairs on my neck stand up stiffer.

Nuh-huh. Nope. I'm not waiting around like some buffet in second hand clothes for whatever nonsense is out there in the wilds. I hitch my backpack high on my shoulders and take off at a jog.

Thump. Thump. Thump.

Damn it. Why did I never do cardio in my whole twenty years? The air wheezes through my tight throat as I push myself on, thin boot soles slapping against the tarmac. I keep scanning the landscape as I jog, running through a mental list of all the contents of my backpack. Trying to think what I could use as a weapon, if it came down to it.

My balled-up socks? Nope.

My toothbrush? Maybe. Sure would hurt if it were shoved in your eye.

I'm so busy scanning and planning that I nearly miss it. The trail of smoke curling up next to the treeline. I slow down, squinting, and the thing is so well camouflaged that I *still* nearly lose it.

A building. A *cabin.* Tucked up flush to the trees, looking out over the wildflowers. It's too far to spy whether someone's home, but that trail of smoke must come from somewhere, right? I chew on the inside of my cheek, weighing up the distance. The knotty tangle of long grass and brush between here and there.

I glance down the tarmac. Both ways; left and right.

There's nothing. Only golden afternoon sunshine and an empty landscape.

And the shiver that skates down my arms.

No, there's *something* out here. Something or someone is

driving my senses haywire. And if my choices are to risk this creepy-ass road for much longer, or try my luck on that mystery cabin, well...

I plunge off the tarmac into thigh-high wildflowers, wrinkling my nose as clouds of pollen rise up and tickle my nostrils. It's like wading through a lake, and if I could curse out loud, you can sure I'd be turning the air blue. It's slow, and hard going, and my ankle rolls in my boot, sharp pain slicing up my leg, and I *still* keep going.

I—I can't explain it. But by halfway, I'm so scared, I'm blinking away tears. Each step, I push faster, farther, gripping my backpack straps until my knuckles turn white. Long grass swishes around my hips, and two separate birds explode out of nowhere, hurtling towards the sky and making me jump out my skin.

By the time I reach the cabin, I'm too far gone for *polite*. I hammer on that front door for all I'm worth, pounding with my fist and slapping open handed against the wood.

I wish I could scream. Cry out.

God. I thump harder. Faster. Let my damp forehead drop against the rattling wood.

When the door wrenches open, pulled by a mountain of a man, I don't wait for him to start yelling. I duck under his huge arm, scurrying inside the dim cabin, and grab a log of firewood to hold like a bat.

Cole

What on God's green earth just shot through my door?

There's a girl in my cabin. No—a woman. A scrap of a thing, wielding a lump of firewood like she wants to knock my head off. Except—except she's not looking at me. She's staring wild-eyed out into the meadows, shifting her weight and biting her lip hard enough to draw blood.

I frown. Turn and peer out into the landscape. Looks the same as it did an hour ago, minus the moose—nothing obvious that might have spooked her. We get wolves in these parts, and a single girl walking alone might tempt a pack. But it's late afternoon, and there's no sign of movement.

No sign of *anything*. Weird.

"You walking on the road?" My voice is gravelly from lack of use. When was the last time I spoke out loud to another person? I wrack my brain, but I can't even remember it. Must have been the supply store in the town. Something like that.

The girl nods, eyes still fixed on the outside. I sigh and close the door.

She stiffens then, a different kind of nervous, but what's the play here? What am I supposed to do? Send her back out into whatever whispering breeze spooked her, never mind her pink cheeks wet with tears?

But the second the door snicks shut, she notices we're alone. That I'm a strange man, gruff and bearded and three times her size to boot. Her eyes flick around the cabin—to the windows, to the poker resting near the fire—but I'm not offended.

She's right to be nervous. What if I'd been a bad man?

You can't go trusting just anyone. Some people are cruel. And a young woman like her, ripe and youthful, with those soft curves and those big, soulful eyes...

"You can go." She flinches again. So I can't be *that* scary, right? If the thought of leaving makes her recoil? "Or stay a while. But the door's not locked. Just so you know." I hold up my palms like I'm surrendering a weapon, hugging the wall as I walk away from the door. I give her a clear shot at the exit, no funny business, and as soon as I reach my kitchen corner, I swipe a pot and set to filling it with water.

Coffee. I'll give her coffee. Then I'll send her on her way.... wherever *that* may be.

"Where are you walking to?" I frown at her over my shoulder. She's placing the log back on the pile, neat and careful. She jerks up when I speak, wiping the wood dust on the front of her jeans, and shrugs. "You don't know?"

She shakes her head.

That can't be right. No one's *that* stupid. And this girl's no fool, you can tell from her quick eyes and quicker thinking. She made it inside my cabin, didn't she? She's getting coffee for her trouble, too.

So either she's lying, or there's something strange happening here. Either way, I should have left my door closed.

I don't like liars *or* fools. And though she's pretty as a picture, the prettiest sight I've seen in—well, my whole life, I won't put up with any bullshit.

"Listen." I place the full pot down with a thud. "You've got five seconds to tell me your deal. Or you're out."

She stares at me, fingers picking at her jeans for way past her five seconds, then blows out a hard breath and starts rooting in her backpack. I watch her, wary. I've got nothing worth stealing in this cabin, but if she's got a gun—

She straightens up. A notebook and pen are clutched in her hands. My gut's already sinking as she picks her way between the log burner and my sofa, dodging the hand-carved coffee table. She comes right up to me, fearless little thing, and flips her notebook open.

I catch a glimpse of the first pages. They're filled with spaced out questions and phrases, written big enough for someone else to read. Printed in a careful hand, things like: *What time is the next bus?* and *A coke, please.*

"Ah, jeez." I scrub the back of my neck, a warm flush tickling my cheeks. Did I have to go and snap at her like that? Tell her to start talking or get out, when it doesn't seem she can? It's classic Cole. Foot: meet mouth.

This is why *I* don't talk much.

She ignores me, flipping through until she finds a blank page, then uncaps her pen with her teeth. She holds the lid balanced between those pearly whites, the pink tip of her tongue poking between her lips, and shit, am I really getting worked up over this?

Fell asleep on the bus. Looking for somewhere to stay and work.

"You want a job?" She nods. I scratch my beard. "There's

the hunting lodge up the road. They take on staff to clean the rooms. But it's half a day's walk away."

Her shoulders slump. She frowns out of the window, annoyed.

"You come from the town?"

She nods, still staring in the direction of the road like it did her wrong.

"Then why'd you come all the way out here?"

She turns that frown on me. A shiver runs up my back, even as a smirk tugs at my mouth. When was the last time I smiled? It feels foreign on my face. Makes my cheeks ache.

She taps the notepad, hard, where it says about falling asleep on the bus. Poor thing. Now that I look at her, she *does* look tired. Dark shadows bruise the underside of her eyes, and her cheeks are hollowed with exhaustion. If I send her back out there like this, she'd be easy pickings.

For man or beast or weather. You name it. Something flares to life in my chest—a fierce protective urge. I can't let that happen.

"Stop over here," I hear myself saying before my brain can catch up. "I'll drive you into town in the morning."

She sucks in a quick breath. Searches my face, her eyes probing, but I've got nothing to hide. I spread my hands and shrug.

"Or head out when you're ready. Your call. But the fire and the food is in here. A hot bath too if you want it."

That brightens her up. When she smiles, it's like a light bulb pings on inside her. And my stomach flips in response.

"Don't get your hopes up," I warn her, squeezing past and leading her to the back door. Maybe if I keep talking, keep us *both* distracted, it won't be so clear I'm tying myself in knots

206

over her. "This isn't the Ritz. The tub's out back. And I'll have to heat the water, so it'll be a while."

Her little hand lands on my forearm and squeezes gently. My heart leaps in my chest.

Oh, lord. She's going to wreck me, I can feel it coming. She's going to turn me inside out. I clear my throat hard and leave her there to poke around, stomping back to the stove to put more water on to boil.

I'll have to fetch more tomorrow. Doesn't matter.

I'll be a good host. Then tomorrow, I'll drop her back in town and wave her on her way.

Harlow

This cabin and the man inside it are like something from a fairy tale. Tucked away and hidden by the trees, where it makes no sense for there to be a home. Out here, where there's just a whole load of nothing.

Inside the cabin is even more story-book. The log burner's crackling away, merrily spreading warmth after the chill of outside, and the air is tinged with wood smoke. There doesn't seem to be any power or running water, and the space is all one big room. There's a gas-lit stove and kitchen counter against one wall; a big bed with a patchwork bedspread against another. A squashy sofa and a simple coffee table. A bookshelf. A square table and two chairs.

As I stroll around his cabin, the questions line up in my brain, faster than I could ever write. So many that my hand would cramp.

Who is this guy? Why does he live out here? Does anyone else live here with him? Does he have a wife?

My eyes flick to the second chair by the table, something

pinching in my stomach. I've only known this man for a few minutes, but I don't like that thought. Because maybe he's big and rough and scary-looking, but it couldn't be clearer from his actions that he's a gentle giant. Hell, he seems more wary of me than I am of him. I get the sure feeling that if I went for him—tried to hit him with that log—he'd stand there and let me do it.

Before he bundled me under his arm and marched me outside. I stifle a smile, running a fingertip along his bookshelf.

He really is big. Bet he could lift me easy as that. Carry me around on his shoulder if he wanted to. And he's older than me, sure, but he's not *that* old. There are faint lines around his eyes, but he's nothing like that crusty neighbor back home.

Not home. I don't have one of those anymore. My heart sinks and I frown at the bookshelf, reading the titles to distract myself.

Wildflowers of the Arctic Circle. Principles of Foraging. The Adventures of Sherlock Holmes.

That last one makes me blink. I spin around to grin at the man, and find him leaning against the counter already watching me. He shrugs, rueful, that blush creeping back over his cheeks above his dark beard.

I love that blush. I want to bring it out brighter. I want to see where else it goes.

"Even I get bored out here sometimes." His voice is rough. Unpracticed. Like he doesn't talk much. Does that mean there's no wife? He pushes off the counter and walks over to join me, peering at his books. "Third load of water's heating. Your bath won't be much longer."

I fumble for my notebook, crammed in my waistband, and uncap my pen.

Thank you. What's your name?

He reads it and winces, shaking his head.

"I'm no good at his, am I? It's Cole." He huffs a sigh, and I don't know why but seeing him down on himself makes my chest ache. He goes to turn away, go back across the cabin, and I grab his sleeve. Tug for him to stay a moment.

My pen scratches over the paper.

I like reading too.

He grunts, eyes flicking to me. They're deep blue, an indigo color, and they rake over my body like he can't help it. I'm not offended. I return the favor, taking him in from his head to his boots.

He's solid. Sculpted. A mountain of muscle, wrapped in a plaid flannel shirt. It'd take two of my hands to wrap all the way around his wrist. My neck aches when I tilt my head back to look at him.

He stares back at me, eyes burning.

I drop my head quickly. Scribble something else; *anything* else.

I'm Harlow.

Even though he didn't ask. Is that awkwardness, or because he doesn't care? Because I'll be gone tomorrow, and he won't spare me another thought?

Cole leans over, reading what I've written, and I get a waft of his scent. Wood smoke and mountain springs.

"Harlow," he rumbles, and yeah, I like that. The sound of my name in his deep voice. The way he says it, like a caress. Shivers skate over my skin, but it's nothing like earlier. They feel good. Tingly. "Nice to meet you, Harlow."

I can't reply, so I do the first thing I think of. I push up onto my toes, place a hand on his shoulder, and kiss his bristly cheek. He bows he head to let me do it, holding his breath, and *god*, I just want to climb him. Loop my arms around his neck and wrap my legs around his middle.

I rock back down on my heels. He swallows, his throat bobbing, eyes hooded and fixed on me. Then he gives himself a little shake and the moment's over. Cole turns away, heading back to the stove.

A bath. I focus on that instead of the nerves fluttering in my stomach. Instead of the sudden slick heat between my legs. It's been three days of traveling. Of the same sweaty clothes and no chance to wash. Of aching muscles and stiff joints.

A bath sounds like heaven.

And a bath drawn for me by Cole, by this gentle mountain giant who looks at me now and then like he longs for all manner of sin... I bite my lip, smiling at his turned away shoulders.

Too bad the bathtub's out back, really. I wouldn't mind if he watched me in it.

* * *

"Here." Cole pours the last steaming vat of water into the tub. It's halfway full—enough to reach my waist, maybe, when I sit down. He scratches his beard, mouth twisting as he looks at the water level. "Sorry it's not more. We need to keep some water back for drinking."

We're out on the back deck. There's a big metal tub, a wooden stool, a shovel leaning against the wall, and a stack of firewood piled neatly undercover. Out between the nearest trees, there's a stump with a hatchet buried in it for chopping wood. The wind whispers through the branches, rustling the leaves, scented with snow off the mountains.

I nudge Cole and smile. He smiles back down at me, relieved, his indigo eyes crinkling at the corners. The breeze tugs his short black hair, and my fingers itch to run through it. To grab handfuls and tug.

"Alright. Well. I'll give you some privacy. Shout if you—" he cuts off, wincing. "Bang on the wall if you need anything." He places a bar of white soap and a wash cloth on the stool beside the tub, along with a folded sage green bath towel.

I catch his wrist before he leaves and rise up to kiss his cheek. Can't stop doing that now I've started. *Especially* since he goes still as a statue every time, holding his breath like he doesn't want to spook me away.

I'm not spooked. I'm—I'm greedy for him. For every detail of his cabin; for his low, steady voice saying my name; for the flashes of desperate hunger in his eyes when he looks at me.

Cole grunts, tearing himself away like it hurts him. His boots thud heavy on the deck as he strides back inside.

When was the last time I undressed outdoors? Maybe swimming in the creek near my uncle's house, back before my body changed? I tug my clothes off quickly, their fabric stiff with dried sweat, sighing with relief as the cold breeze kisses my bare skin.

The water's warm. Steam curls off the surface, dancing up towards the eaves of the cabin, and I bite my lip as I lower myself into the tub. Every aching muscle, every sore joint—they all sing out with joy as I lay back in the water. In *Cole's* water. The bath that he drew me.

I lie there for way too long. My eyelids flutter closed, and I lie in the warm, silky water, dreaming of the man inside his cabin, just a few feet away. And only when it's gone cool, when

I've started to shiver, nipples beading, do I sit up and snatch the soap and wash cloth off the stool.

I can't be ungrateful. But as I scrub away the grime of the last few days, I can't help but wish there were three more baths waiting. At least—at least I won't smell bad now. If Cole comes near.

God, please let him come near.

A twig snaps in the forest. The hollow crack echoes through the trees, and I freeze, soapy washcloth dragged halfway up one arm. I scan the trees, heart thundering, but there's nothing. *Nothing.* And yet...

The hairs rise on the back of my neck.

Cole. I drop the soap and washcloth with a splash, lurching up out of the tub. I don't care that I'm naked, don't care that I'm still soapy, don't care about anything except getting back inside. I hammer on the cabin door, panic ringing in my ears, until it yanks open and I fall into Cole's chest.

"What the—it was open, Harlow. What are you..." He registers that I'm naked. Wet and trembling. Clinging to him, half sick with fear. Cole curses, crushing me closer with one arm and snagging the towel off the stool with the other, then swaddles me quickly, wrapping me up while his eyes stay fixed on the trees. "There something out there, honey?"

I nod, face pressed into his shirt.

"Alright. Go on inside. I'm going to take a look, okay?"

I shake my head, hard. Bunch my fingers in his shirt. The thought of him leaving me alone, going out there where I can't follow, it's... I screw my eyes shut. I can't breathe.

"Easy, Harlow. I'll just be two minutes. Get on inside and get warmed up."

There's nothing for it. He scoops me up and carries me

inside, putting me down gently in front of the log burner. The heat licks at my bare legs, sudden and intense, and he tips up my chin.

"Two minutes. I promise."

His boots shake the cabin floor as he strides out the back exit. And I clutch the ends of my thin towel closer, watching him go.

Cole

There's something out here, alright. Harlow's no fool. If my girl says there's something following her, there's something following her. I shut the cabin door behind me, gritting my teeth before spinning the key in the lock.

Hopefully she trusts me by now. If not, I'll have some explaining to do when I come back.

My steps are silent once I leave the deck, padding over the dirt and grass into the trees. I pause at the chopping stump, yanking my hatchet loose.

I'm not a violent man, but you can't be too careful. And when it comes to Harlow... who knows. I have a feeling I'd do *anything* to keep her safe.

If Harlow's word weren't enough—which it is—the birds would be a clue. They're silent. Still. Watching and waiting. Which means there's something moving through these trees that shouldn't be here. Something or someone.

I scan the forest floor as I walk, searching for signs of life. Dropped scat. Scuffed boot prints. Anything. But there's nothing out of place in the trees, nor out in the wildflower meadow when I circle the cabin. If my ears weren't registering the eerie silence, I'd think everything was normal.

I don't like it.

"No sign." I spin the lock of the front door too once I let myself back in. We're sealed in fully now, but it doesn't freak her out like earlier. Over by the log burner, Harlow looks relieved. She's still wrapped in a towel, her dark hair wet down her back, and there are soap bubbles sitting on her damp skin.

No. That won't do. I place the hatchet down on the table and cross to grab a dish cloth from the kitchen. I dunk it in the water and wring it out before bringing it back.

"Here. Clean the rest off." I offer her the cloth, but Harlow bites her lip and looks up at me. Her cheeks flush as she turns her body, showing me her soapy arm.

Damn. Well. This wasn't my plan, but I sure as hell won't pass up a chance to touch her.

"Nothing's coming in here," I tell her as I drag the cloth over her bare skin. Goosebumps ripple in my wake, and I swallow hard. "The doors are locked. And even if they weren't, I'm a big motherfucker. Anything coming for you would have to go through me."

Her breath shudders out of her. She nods, darting me a quick smile, then turns and gives me her other arm. I wipe that down too, trying not to think too hard about the parts under her towel.

There's no need to wonder. Harlow answers the question I'd never dare ask, dropping the towel to the ground and turning to give me her back. I grit my teeth and drag the cloth over the smooth expanse of skin, following the line of her waist. Where it nips in; where her hips flare. I don't touch lower down, but I can't help looking at the rounded swell of her ass. The two perfect handfuls, made for squeezing and spreading.

My heavy breathing fills the cabin; tells the awful truth about me. Tells Harlow how badly I want her. She should be disgusted, a sweet young thing like her. She should push me away, judgement harsh in her eyes.

She doesn't do those things. Harlow turns again, eyes bright, and it takes every ounce of my willpower to keep my gaze above her neck. My jaw clenches so tight, I swear my teeth will crack, and I can't do it. Can't touch her perfect body and still be a gentleman. I push the cloth into her hand.

"Finish up," I tell her, voice rough, and is that disappointment clouding her face? But she turns away and does what I said, scrubbing herself clean and scooping the towel up again. She covers her gorgeous body back over, refusing to look at me, and it cracks me open down the middle.

I didn't mean to be harsh. But I don't know how to set this right. How to relax those tensed up shoulders. So I grab her backpack for her and place it by her feet.

"Get dressed. I'll wait outside."

She slumps even further into herself. How am I doing this? What am I saying wrong? Fuck. This is why I live alone out here. I'm not built for—for all this. Talking and reading other people's moods. But Harlow looks so dejected, I have to say *something.* I can't leave her in here when her eyes are downcast like that, brimming with tears.

"You're beautiful." The word scrapes the sides of my throat. "Don't go wasting the sight of that body on me."

The floorboards rattle under my strides, then I'm back out in the safety of the air.

* * *

That ass. Jesus Christ. It'll haunt my dreams. I drag a hand over my face, squinting out towards the road. My heart is slamming hard enough to crack a rib, but it's not from fear. If something came for Harlow right now, I'd tear it into pieces with my bare hands.

No. It's her. She's under my skin, just like that. She's only been here a few hours, and I'm already gone for her. I reach down and palm my hard cock through my jeans, hating myself for it, but I'm so turned on it hurts. I need some relief.

A sound floats through the door. Muffled movement in the cabin. I snatch my hand away, shamed.

She's a runaway. A girl in trouble, seeking shelter. That's all she wants from me. *All* she wants.

I stand out on the deck until I trust myself again. Until my breaths have slowed and the band around my chest loosens an inch. I only step back inside the cabin when the sun set bruises the sky and I'm one hundred percent sure I won't toss her over my shoulder and carry her to the bed.

Harlow's sitting on the sofa. Her arms are wrapped around her legs, her chin resting on her knees. Her eyes flick up when I come in, raking over me from head to toe, but then she licks her lips and drops her gaze.

"Harlow?" She looks up again. Forces a polite smile. God, I hate this. "What's wrong? Did you hear something?" I glare at the windows at the back of the cabin, striding over to peer out into the trees. After a long search, I huff and drag the curtains closed.

If this were full winter, it'd be dark. The sun wouldn't rise, even in the day. Harlow's lucky the seasons are turning, summer fading into the brief fall before winter settles in, or she'd have been stalked in constant nighttime instead. Plunging thigh-deep through thick drifts of snow.

I never cover up my windows. Never lock my doors. Whatever is out there, it's disturbed my goddamn peace. And even worse, it's made Harlow look like this—pale and tired and sad.

She's scribbling in her notebook when I turn back. Neck bent, her hand flying over the page. Bet it sucks when her pen runs out. I should buy a stash. Keep them here just in case.

But no—she's not staying, is she? I'm getting caught up in my thoughts. Confusing dreams for reality.

"That for me?" I call. She nods, still writing, and I sigh and brace myself as I walk back over. It's not that I don't want to be near her—it's that I want it too much. Something about this young woman beats my heart like a drum. And when I lean over, bracing my hands on the back of the sofa, and get a whiff of my soap on her soft skin—

I jerk upright, rubbing the back of my neck. She can pass it up when she's done.

Her pen clicks closed. Harlow crawls around on the sofa, pushing up onto her knees, and I notice that she's wearing one of my shirts, the sleeves rolled about a dozen times. She's wearing leggings too under that, thank god, else I'd have already flattened her onto her back, rutting her into the cushions like a beast.

Harlow holds the notepad against her chest. Shakes it slightly so I'll read. I bend down and peer at it, shame creeping up my throat at how slow I am to read her neat writing. I read it out loud, stilted and rough, so she can know how far I'm getting.

"I'm sorry for dropping my towel."

I break off already, scratching my beard. "Don't be sorry. You didn't... You took me be surprise. That's all." She rolls her eyes and shakes the notebook. Urges me to keep reading.

"I wanted you to see me. I'm sorry for that too." I pinch the bridge of my nose, screwing my eyes shut. My breaths rasp out louder.

"Don't need to apologize for that either." That's all I trust myself to say. And it's not until a hand tugs gently at my sleeve that I force myself to open my eyes and keep reading. I'm rock hard in my jeans, and she must be able to see it, but she's not running out the door. And she must *know* that it's her words doing this to me.

"I want to make you feel good. Will you let me?" My voice cracks. I grit my teeth, tugging the notebook from her hands and flipping it closed. I can't read anymore. Not if I want to keep my sanity intact. She scowls, tugging it back, and flipping through the pages, so I walk away. Talk to the wall as I go.

"You don't owe me that. You don't owe me anything, you hear? You're staying one night, eating some food, then heading out. That's all."

The paging sounds stop behind me. I glance back, but she's wilted. Dropped to sit on her heels, her shoulders slumped in defeat, her notebook held loosely in her lap. I'm trying to protect her, damn it, trying to do the right thing, so why do I feel like the world's biggest asshole?

"It's not..." I swallow hard. Speak with a rasp. "It's a kind offer. And believe me—normally, I would want that. I'd slap myself, not believing my good luck. But you're vulnerable, and you came here for help." I square my shoulders. "I won't take advantage of that."

220

She throws her hands up, exasperated, and starts paging again. And though I'm relieved to see her spirit come back, I'm done reading.

At least until I've got some food in her. Food in us *both*.

God knows I need some strength.

Harlow

Cole wants me. Physically, at least. When I turned to face him, my towel puddled at my feet, I saw the way his chest heaved. The way his fists clenched, tendons standing out on his forearms. And when he read what I'd written, the things I was offering, his pupils blew so wide his eyes turned black.

So why is he being such a freaking brick wall about this? For the next few hours, he barely says a word. He potters around his cabin, fixing us dinner on his gas stove. Won't even *look* at me over his shoulder. As though I might have stripped naked and laid out on the table with an apple in my mouth.

Whatever. I won't force the issue. I'm grateful that he's taken me in, and I'll respect his wishes. But that doesn't stop my body from singing out like a tuning fork whenever he passes near. Doesn't stop the slick warmth from gathering between my legs; the way my pulse thrums every time he mutters under his breath.

I want *him.* At least one of us should be honest. I want him on me and in me; surrounding me so completely that we blur into one.

I chew on my pen cap. Should I write that down?

No point. He won't read it.

As the daylight changes outside the windows, darkness creeping in, Cole adds another log to the burner. It crackles and pops, an ember floating near my sock, and I stare at the flames in a daze.

"Dinner won't be long." I nod and force a smile. He sighs, the sound gusting out of him. I wait, but he doesn't say anything else. Just moves away, floorboards creaking.

Cole is a great cook. I shouldn't be so surprised—it's pretty insulting of me, really. But he's so *big*, his hands dwarfing the knife as he chops, and it's hard to believe he made this stew with these delicate flavors. I spoon it greedily into my mouth, tearing chunks of bread off with my teeth, and Cole watches me wide-eyed before bursting out laughing. He tips back his head and roars at the ceiling, loud enough to scare the birds out in the trees.

"Easy, honey." He reaches over and places a hand on my wrist. Weighs my spoon down. "Don't make yourself sick. There's plenty more, just go slow. Okay?"

I nod, stomach swooping as he watches me, then withdraws his hand. My wrist jerks up at the sudden loss of him. God. What would that weight be like, covering me *everywhere*?

"Oh no, you don't." Cole nudges my bowl closer. "Eat first. One hunger at a time."

That's... that's almost a yes. Right? I blink at him, hope swelling in my chest. Then he shakes his head and sighs, turning back to his own meal, and my heart sinks.

He won't change his mind.

I dip my spoon into the stew and duck my head. I should

take what I'm given and be grateful.

* * *

Two hours later, we're standing shoulder to shoulder, staring at the bed.

"In you get," Cole says gruffly. "Both the doors are locked. I'll sleep on the rug."

Like a dog? No. No way. It's *his bed*, and I could easily sleep on the sofa. Unlike him, I'd fit without spilling off both ends. I scrabble for my notebook, ready to tell him so, but he holds up his palms.

"Please, Harlow. Have mercy. I can't share the bed with you."

If he'd just *listen*—I bury my hands in my hair and pull. If I could talk, speak out loud, he couldn't refuse to hear me this way. Couldn't assume he already knows what I'm trying to say. It's infuriating, so freaking unfair, and though he reaches for me, concerned, I skip out of reach and climb onto the bed.

Fine. He wants to basically gag me? Refuse to read my words? Then I'm done talking to him too.

"Harlow." He steps closer, face clouding over. "What is it? What have I done? What were you going to write?"

I burrow under the covers, rolling onto my side. Stay glaring at the wall until I hear him move away. My teeth are gritted, tears stinging my eyes, but I keep my breathing steady. Won't show him how bad it hurts. The floor creaks as he stretches out on the rug, over by the crackling log burner. For an absurd moment, I worry for him. Worry that an ember will land on him and burn. But it's none of my business, is it?

And even if I wanted to say something, I couldn't. I'd have to write it down and hope he felt like reading it.

I drag the covers over my head and will myself to sleep.

* * *

The sound shocks me awake. A crash out in the trees—sudden and violent. I sit bolt upright in bed, already breathing in shallow gasps, hands scrabbling for the covers pooled in my lap.

"Harlow. Honey. Look at me." There's a warm pressure on my cheek. Cole is cupping my face. He waits until I'm focused on him, until the ringing in my ears has faded enough to hear. "I'm going to take a look. Stay inside and stay quiet. Okay?"

I nod, catching his wrist before he can leave. His pulse races under my fingers, and he hesitates before leaning down and kissing my forehead.

"Stay hidden. Don't open the curtains."

Then he's gone, cold air whistling through the back door before he slams it shut. My head jerks to the table. The hatchet is gone.

Okay. Okay. Cole lives here full time. He must be used to bears and wildlife and creepy noises. I swallow hard, my tongue glued to the roof of my mouth, and stare blindly at the dying embers in the log burner.

Outside, a twig snaps.

God. Oh god. I scramble onto my knees, shuffling along the bed until I reach the window. I don't touch the curtains—I'm not that dumb—but I press my eye close to gap, peering out into the darkness.

It's like another world. My uncle lives pretty far north, but back at his house, the northern lights were a treat. A rare sight, and when they came, they were wispy. Muted.

225

This is something else altogether. Ribbons of green light dance among the stars, rippling and so vivid, they put other colors to shame. They cast an eerie glow over the landscape, tinting the trees and the meadows, and I can only imagine this in deep winter, the light bouncing off thick snow.

A shadow moves between the trees. Cole? I lean closer, my breath fogging the glass. Then the front door slams open, and I jump.

"It's me." He stomps inside. "A branch fell. That's all."

But... I spin and peer through the crack again, but there's nothing there. No shadow. Did I imagine it? I stare harder until my eyes run dry.

"Harlow." Cole's voice comes from beside the bed. He takes me by the shoulders, easing me back down to sit. "If there's something or someone out there, you're safe in here with me. Okay?"

I nod, teeth chattering. I don't know what's wrong with me. I've always held my own—I've had to, growing up as the girl who can't speak. But something about being out here in the wilderness, feeling watched, feeling like *prey*...

I grab Cole by the sleeve and tug him toward the bed.

No funny business. That's what I'd write if my notebook were near. But I don't have to, because this time he sighs and sits down on the mattress. The bed springs creak, the sudden dip jerking me toward him, and *that's* what I want.

His bulk. His safe, soothing presence.

"Alright. Shuffle up." I make room for him. He kicks his boots off, then climbs into bed, jeans and all. It can't be comfortable, but I don't dare push my luck and try to get him to take them off. He'd sprint back to that rug quicker than my heart is racing.

Cole lies down, tense and awkward. And though he grunts when I grab his arm, curling him around me, he scoots closer, plastering himself against my back. He's warm. Solid. He smells so freaking good. Like soap and man and safety.

"What's following you, huh?" he murmurs into my hair. "You tempt Bigfoot?"

I shrug. It's hard to imagine someone bigger than him. And though I'm still shaking, still shivery with fear, it doesn't take long for me to melt back against his chest. After a moment, his palm smooths over my stomach. His fingers slip between the buttons of his borrowed shirt, tracing over my skin. My breath hitches, and I can't help it. I arch back against him, rubbing my ass against the hard length prodding me from behind.

Cole groans and buries his face in my neck. His beard tickles, and I bite my lip hard enough to bleed.

I want him. I want him. I want him so badly.

His teeth scrape over my throat.

"God damn it." He mutters so quietly. Like he's talking to himself. "Can't fucking help it. So sweet. So perfect." His hand gets rougher, going from gentle stroking to kneading. He grips and squeezes every part of me—my hip, my waist, my chest—all while he pants into my neck and ruts at me from behind. I sigh in his grip, a tiny rag doll compared to him, and it's *everything*. Everything I've been craving.

I reach back, tentative, and scrabble for his belt. His hand slams down over mine, trapping my fingers against his buckle.

"Wait." His chest heaves against my back. No, no, no, *how* did I throw him off again? But then he sits up, rummaging around for my notebook, and pushes it and the pen into my hands.

"Write it down, honey. Tell me what you want. More important, tell me what you *don't* want." There's enough light still from the log burner to see. I flick through the pages, fingers shaking.

I steal a glimpse of him, and my breath seizes in my chest. He's wild. Wrecked. Barely restrained. His eyes are dark and glinting, his cheeks flushes and his hair mussed. He looks about ready to *eat* me.

I want it all. My letters are wobbly. The pen stabs through the paper. *All of it. I want you inside me.*

Cole stills when he reads that. He turns to stone on the bed, and I'm about to prod his shoulder when he sucks in a shuddering breath. He comes back to life, taking the pen and notebook and placing them carefully on the nightstand.

"Here." He takes my hand. Wraps my fingers into a fist. "You want to stop, you knock. Okay?" He knocks my fist gently against the wall to demonstrate. Then against his shoulder. His head. I grin, tugging at his beard when he lets me go. He tips my chin up. "Promise me, honey."

I hold his gaze. Draw a cross over my heart.

Cole

I don't know what I did in a past life to deserve this, but whatever it was, I'd better do it again. Because now that I've tasted Harlow, now that I've felt her soft skin under my callused palms, I can never go back.

So I'd better get to work, deserving her. Burrowing under her skin the way she's already under mine. She shuffles back on the mattress, biting her lip and staring at me before whipping my shirt over her head.

Just like that. My Harlow's a firecracker. She bides her time, figures out what she wants, then: *boom*. I never stood a chance.

Her body is as pale and curvy and perfect as the glimpse I got earlier, the sight burned into my brain. But this time, I don't look away, shame gripping my throat. This time, I let myself look my fill.

She's bare. No bra, just those perky tits, small but gorgeous with rosy pink nipples. Dark brown moles dot her skin, the cutest constellation, and a pink flush creeps down her chest. Harlow frowns at me—not mad, just determined—and cups her tits. Squeezes them in challenge.

"Oh, honey." I crawl forward, flattening her back against the bed. She blinks up at me, her tongue darting out to wet her lips. "You don't have to tempt me anymore. It's done. I won't stop now until you knock, or until I've pumped that sweet pussy full." Her breath hitches at the way I'm talking to her, dirty and low, and she winds her arms around my neck.

"That's right, baby girl. Touch me wherever you want."

I didn't think she was holding back. She's been bold since she got here, always tugging on my sleeve and kissing my cheek. But those words set something loose in her. She smirks, sudden and fierce, then lunges up to tug me down. Makes me flatten her whole body with mine. I go to push myself up—I don't want to crush her—but she's *writhing*. Panting hot little breaths against my neck.

"You like being weighed down, Harlow? You like being trapped under a man?"

She nips my earlobe. Pokes my cheek. And it's clear that she's saying: *Not 'a man'. Trapped under you.* My heart swells at that, big enough to burst my rib cage, but she's huffing and rubbing herself on me like a cat. Hooking her leg around my hip and arching up against me.

I've got work to do.

"These pretty leggings are in the way." I flick the waistband. She reaches between us, wriggling them down. I smooth a hand over her ass, expecting panties, but there's *nothing*.

Fuck. I swat her ass. "You're a goddamn tease, aren't you?"

She nods, catching my hand and dragging it to her pussy. Harlow's not messing around. And when I touch her there I see why: she's soaking wet, her pussy pulsing, and only the lightest graze of my thumb over her clit makes her twitch.

"So fucking responsive." I don't know who I'm muttering to. Me or her. "I bet you could come so easy, baby. I bet I could blow on your pussy and you'd fall apart."

She's nodding, tugging at my wrist, writhing like she's in pain, and suddenly I can't take it either. I break her hold on me easily, sliding both hands under her ass, then push up to kneel and lift her with me in one motion. She gasps, knees locking around my neck, and I lick a broad stripe up her slit. Hold her to my mouth and feast on her like a starving man.

Goddamn. She tastes good. Sweet and musky and ready. Begging out to be stretched by a cock. Harlow scrabbles for the bed covers, grabbing fistfuls of sheets as I work her in long, messy licks.

I'm not a delicate man. I don't do fancy techniques. What I *do*, is eat her pussy like it's the best thing I've ever tasted. Wild and eager, until she's slicked all over my face. And only once her muscles clench, her stomach shuddering as she comes, do I give her one last lick and settle her down on the bed.

Lord, she's a sight. Red faced and hair mussed. Even now, limp and breathless, she still reaches for me. I run a fingertip up and down her pink slit, not dipping inside.

"You want a cock in here, honey?"

Another poke. *Your cock.* I grin, savage triumph singing through my chest. But when I press my finger to the first knuckle, I feel how tight she is. How untried.

"Fuck." I scrub a hand over my beard and ask her straight. "You done this before?"

She pauses. I can *see* her deciding whether to lie. Then she shakes her head with a tiny jerk. I suck in a deep breath, heart thudding out a war beat.

"And you're sure, honey? You want it to be me?"

She smiles, then soft and relieved. Like she thought I'd turn her away.

As if I could. I'm not so saintly.

"This might hurt," I warn her, unbuckling my belt. She stares at me hungrily as I shed my clothes. I'm big and hairy and brutish next to her, but I can't deny the flush it brings to her cheeks. The way she squeezes her thighs together, squirming on the mattress. "You remember to knock if you want to stop. Okay?"

A huff. An impatient nod. So I'm smiling when I push her thighs apart. When I settle between her legs and notch myself against her. She's so damn small—I can span her rib cage with one hand—so I grunt and flip us over. Her shocked breath turns to a scowl, but she settles into my lap, resting her palms on my chest.

"It'll hurt less this way. You're in control."

Because I don't trust myself not feel a single inch of her pussy, then lose my mind. Thrust clean inside and rut at her like a wild animal. Something tells me Harlow would like that another day, but right now... it's time to be gentle.

I can do that. I'd rather die than cause her pain.

"Line yourself up." She does as I say, her little hand wrapping around my cock. I groan at just that contact, thrusting up into her palm.

Yeah. It's better she's on top.

Harlow notches my broad tip against her entrance. Gives a cute little wiggle, trying it out for size.

"It's big, huh?" I'm not trying to brag. I'm trying to brace her. Warn her what's coming.

She nods, but there's a fierce set to her jaw. My Harlow's a fighter.

She sinks down the first inch fast, gritting her teeth. Her nails dig into my chest. She breathes hard and slow.

"That's it. Catch your breath, baby girl. Let your pussy stretch."

She tips her head back, closing her eyes. After a long moment, she licks her bottom lip. Starts moving her hips again. Harlow rides the head of my cock—just the head, nothing else—and only that makes my balls swell and draw close to my body. I clench my jaw too, willing myself not to spill. To make this good for her. To give her the first time she deserves.

"Take another inch," I tell her hoarsely, running my palms up her thighs. I'm trying to be good for her here, but I'm only human. And this is an insane pussy, the best thing I've ever felt, and *god*, when she sinks down further I nearly blow.

"Wait. Honey, wait." She stills, face bemused. Then when she realizes why I've stopped her, wicked amusement fills her eyes. She rocks her hips again, harder than before, and grins, delighted, when I let out a rough groan. I swat her ass, cursing and squeezing my eyes shut.

I open them again. I don't want to miss a second of this.

"Harlow," I rasp. "You're going to tip me over." She pushes down on my dick harder, taking more of it inside her. There are only a couple inches left now, and the sight of her pussy spread around me—"Fuck." I tear my eyes away.

Harlow's still grinning. She loves this, the little tease. Loves having me weak and under her control. She reaches over and scratches her fingernails through my beard. Sucks in a sharp breath when I nip at her thumb.

"Harlow," I warn. She sighs and pushes down, taking the final inch inside her. When her ass hits my thighs, she rolls her hips, swirling my cock in her pussy. *"Harlow."*

Her breath huffs out of her as she laughs. She tweaks her nipples and smiles at me, suddenly shy.

"Perfect," I tell her, covering her hands with my own. Kneading her tits. "So goddamn perfect."

This time, when she starts to move, she builds up a slow rhythm. Her forehead pinches in concentration as she rises up then falls, rises then falls. I slide in and out of her, her wetness easing the way, and I feel every inch of that friction zap through my body. I lay still at first, but after a minute, I can't help it. I thrust up against her, hips rising to meet her.

"Harlow." I say her name like a prayer. "Come for me. Come on my cock."

She bounces against my lap, thighs trembling, nodding and squeezing her eyes shut, and when I rub her clit, her breath stalls in her lungs. She shakes something fierce, the waves tearing through her little body, her pussy clamping down on me so hard my ears ring. And I snarl, working her clit until she slumps forward, boneless. Then bury myself to the hilt and pour everything inside her.

Our ragged breaths fill the cabin. We lie in the dying firelight, sticky and flushed hot but grinning.

"Harlow." She rubs her nose in my chest hair. My laugh rumbles into her. "Let me up. I'll clean us off."

It's the least I can do. And besides, I want to take care of her. Meeting her needs, providing for her—it soothes me somewhere, deep inside.

Don't get used to it, a voice whispers in my head. Because she's a runaway. Just passing through.

Harlow may have waltzed in here and exploded my world. Turned my whole existence upside down. But tomorrow morning, I've promised to drive her to town. Then god knows where she'll go after.

I roll off the bed, pain throbbing in my chest.

There's nothing I can offer her here.

Harlow

I wake up with a fierce ache between my legs, and a steady pulse there too. It's ironic—my body wants Cole badly, even though last night hurt just as much as it felt good. And my heart is no better.

I roll onto my side, watching him cook at the stove top. He's dressed in dark pants, boots, and a green checked shirt, the fabric straining over his wide shoulders. The smell of bacon and eggs wafts through the cabin, and my stomach growls loud enough to bring down the roof.

Cole smirks at me over his shoulder. "Someone's hungry."

His eyes flick over my body, lingering. Then he turns back to the pan.

That's it.

I nibble on my thumbnail, pushing to sit up. It's cold outside the covers, even with the log burner crackling away, and when I turn and peer at the window I find frost lacing the glass. The shadow I saw between the trees last night flickers across my mind, and I push up onto my knees to peer through the gap in the curtain.

Nothing. Pale trees in the cool wash of dawn. I settle back onto the mattress, head spinning.

Cole promised he'd drive me to town. That's what he offered me: one night, some food, and a ride in the morning. After last night, I thought maybe... maybe something had changed. Maybe he wouldn't be so quick to rush me out the door.

His back to me stamps out that hope. Cole might like me, might have enjoyed what we did, but nothing's changed. He still wants me gone.

I eat my bacon and eggs on the front deck, my plate balanced on my knees, staring out at the wildflowers. There's no creeping dread this morning. No hairs standing up on my neck. Only bright, swaying flowers and pain slicing through my chest.

I can't go. I can't leave him.

But he won't ask me to stay.

The food tastes like ashes in my mouth, never mind that it's cooked to perfection. I force myself to eat it all anyway, swallowing every last bite—god knows when I'll have another square meal again. I have nothing. Not a dollar to my name. And today, I've got to go out there and beg a job. Start a new life.

A life away from Cole. Will it be worse, knowing he's a few hours away? Will he ever visit?

I sniffle, wiping my nose on my sleeve. And crap—this isn't my shirt. Is this really how I'm going to thank him?

"Keep it." Cole sounds amused behind me. His footsteps vibrate the deck, then he's easing down to sit beside me. He rests his wrists on his knees, squinting at the snow-capped mountains in the distance. "I'll give you a few things to take with you. Some clothes. Food. Cash."

I'm not too proud for his charity. I've always been pragmatic. And I know my situation is dire. But it's worse, somehow, to have him take care of me like this. From arm's length. Like I'm any other cause.

I nod, setting the plate on the deck and resting my chin on my knees. I should thank him, but my notebook is inside. And he must sense the sadness filling me up to the brim, because Cole sighs and smooths his palm over my hair.

"It's okay, Harlow. You're a brave girl. You'll be fine." I squeeze my eyes shut tight, tears brimming.

I know that I'm brave. I know I'll be fine. But since I first knocked on his door, that's not enough anymore. I've felt what it's like to be wanted; treasured and safe. To have someone *understand* me, for the first time in my life.

How am I supposed to give that up?

"Come on." Cole pushes to his feet. "I'll start the truck."

It doesn't matter. The choice isn't mine.

* * *

The truck pulls up to the sidewalk, the engine cutting out. We're back in town—if you can call it that. It's more like a single road, dotted with basic shops and a few cafes on either side. Further out, there's a gas station in the distance. What looks like a motel. I guess the people who live here live out in cabins like Cole's. Hidden in the landscape.

"Well." Cole scratches his beard, staring out the driver's window. He won't look at me. I wait for a few seconds, but he's really not going to turn. Not going to tell me goodbye.

I huff and shove my door open, hopping down onto the

sidewalk and placing the note I wrote him on the seat. It's not like he deserves it after not even looking at me, but I meant it all. So. Whatever.

I drum my fingers on the side of the truck. He clears his throat.

"Bye, honey." Doesn't even turn his head.

I slam the truck door hard enough that the glass rattles. I'm being so rude, so ungrateful, but it *hurts* that he won't look. That I might never feel those dark eyes on me again. I shoulder my backpack in a daze, so much heavier now that it's stuffed full of Cole's supplies. And I start walking.

It's early morning, still. Most places aren't open. So I point my feet at the motel in the distance, figuring I'll start looking for work there. I push my legs to move faster, blood pumping, flushing hot with how we left things. With how *Cole* left things.

I thought maybe...

He loved me.

That's crazy. I know that. It's a stupid thing to think after one night. But the worse thing is, I already love him. I know I do, right down to the marrow in my bones. Cole is written over my insides, the way I write in my notebook. Cut me open, and you'll find his name etched on my ribs.

And he wouldn't even look at me to say goodbye. I sniff hard, scrubbing angrily at the tears on my cheeks. My boots thud against the sidewalk, the motel looming bigger as I get near. It's worn down. Tired. Beat-up by the cold and wind.

Well, that's okay. I am too.

* * *

I slap the bell on the front desk, wincing as the shrill sound pierces the air. I'll piss them off before I've even begun. A middle-aged woman with wiry dark hair bustles through a doorway, all business, no nonsense.

"Yes?"

I nudge my piece of paper across the desk. She leans down and reads it, her mouth pressed in a line.

"No. Sorry. I don't hire now until the summer." The woman glances over me—at my threadbare coat. My holey jeans. My red eyes. Her mouth softens, and she really does look sorry. She's softer when she says, "Come back in the spring. Okay?"

I nod, heart sinking. What am I supposed to do until then? Wait in the parking lot all winter? I tug my backpack higher on my shoulders and push back outside. Back to try my luck somewhere else.

I'm halfway back to town when I feel it. The hairs rise on the back of my neck. Except I've been so wrapped up in my misery, staring down at my boots, that he's already on me, hand clapping over my mouth.

"There you are." The man breathes hot on my neck. His voice is familiar, and I struggle against his grip. But he's bigger than me, and stronger, and he took me by surprise, trapping my arms against my body. "I've been watching you."

I grunt and wrench to the left, peering around wild-eyed, and I see him: the hunter who drove past me by the bus stop. Who offered me a ride. He's red-faced and rigid, spit flecking his lip, and his mouth curls into a snarl as he drags me towards his truck. I kick and thrash, dragging my feet over the road, but he curses and pulls me harder.

"Don't make this harder for yourself." I bite at his hand, teeth sinking into flesh. He roars and tears his hand away, and I spit his blood onto the ground. "Bitch!"

His palm cracks against my cheekbone. Tilts the world sideways and makes my head spin. I drop to my knees, ears ringing, and it takes a minute for sounds to fade back in. For my vision to stop swimming. Then I see it.

Cole, holding the man by the neck. Punching him so hard, his body goes limp.

Cole, stepping over the hunter and crouching in front of me. His panicked indigo eyes, his gentle hands cradling my face.

"Harlow? Honey. Can you hear me?"

I force myself to nod. Bile surges in my throat. Cole holds me even as I turn and vomit. Even as spot of it land on his boots. He rubs my back, up and down between my shoulder blades, murmuring about how I'll be okay.

I don't feel okay. I feel dizzy. My cheekbone throbs hot. And—and that man *grabbed* me. Tried to drag me away. I wipe my mouth on my sleeve and bury my face in Cole's chest.

I already saved myself from my uncle. Can't I catch a break?

"Alright. I've got you." Cole pushes to his feet, scooping me up into his arms. He carries me like a child, my legs wrapped around his waist and my face tucked away in this throat. His beard tickles my nose.

What happens now? Is there a police station around here? Is he going to drop me back at a cafe or something to ask for a job?

But no—Cole carries me back to his truck. Bundles me into the passenger seat, clipping my seat belt in place.

"I read your note." His voice is rough. So intense it cracks. "I love you too, honey. I'm so sorry I let you go like that. Let that—that *lowlife* put his hands on you."

I turn in the seat. Stare out the back window up the road.

The man's body is slumped on the tarmac. Still not moving.

"Yeah." Cole coughs. "I might have done some damage there." I look over at him for the first time since he scooped me up. He's chalky white, his eyes haunted. He looks *wrecked*. "You still want to come home with me, Harlow? Even after seeing that? Even after I let you down so bad?"

I nod so hard my teeth rattle. Cole didn't let me down. He's *never* let me down—not when it counts. He hurt my feelings, sure, but when I piece the morning back together, picture it from his point of view, his heart breaking too, just like mine...

Yes, I want to go home with him. I never want to leave again.

And he sighs, broken and ragged, pressing a bristly kiss to my temple.

"Perfect girl. I'll make this up to you. For the rest of our lives."

Cole

Two Years Later

I pull the truck to a stop outside the motel, killing the engine and sitting in the quiet. This is the best part of my day: seeing her again for the first time. It's only been a few hours apart, but my heart still thumps like crazy every time.

Harlow pushes out of the motel doors, waving goodbye to her boss. She's smiling bright, the little light bulb switched on inside her, and she practically skips as she crosses to the truck.

Good. That's all I care about. That my wife is happy and safe.

"Seat belt," I grunt as soon as she's settled in her seat. She rolls her eyes, but I catch the tug at the corner of her mouth.

Harlow loves that I worry about her. That I fuss over her, desperate to see to her every need.

Just as well. It's only going to get worse, now that her belly is swelling with our child. Harlow smooths her palms over the bump, her smile dreamy as I pull the truck back into the road.

She doesn't notice anything's up until I turn right instead of left. Back toward town instead of home to our cabin.

She doesn't nudge me or raise an eyebrow. Must think we're picking up supplies, but when we blow through town without stopping, *then* she turns to me, forehead creased.

"Got something to show you," I say gruffly. She flicks my shoulder and I grin. "Be patient. Little brat."

Her huffed laugh makes my pulse race. She always does this—floors me with every sly expression. Every flick of her hair. So when I finally pull off the road onto a dirt track, I can't help darting little glances at her. I want to soak up every reaction. Make sure she really likes this surprise.

If she doesn't, I'll tear it down and start over.

Her gasp whispers through the truck as we round a bend. It comes into view: our new cabin.

It's nothing crazy. I'm still Cole and she's Harlow. It's not like either of us has been dreaming of a mansion. But with the baby coming, and with the way she loves her baths so much, I figured…

Time for a little luxury.

Luxury in mountain terms, anyway. Electricity. Wifi. Hot running water. All the things that Harlow has never complained about missing, but that I wanted to give her anyway. She grabs my sleeve, thumping my shoulder as we pull up outside.

"It's nothing special," I warn her as I kill the engine. "So don't—don't get your hopes up. But there's a bathroom with running water and a proper kitchen and electricity—"

She cuts me off, her mouth crushing against mine. I groan and gather her close, flicking open her seat belt and pulling her into my lap. The truth is, our new home *is* special. I got the best materials, hired the best help. Did a lot of the work with my bare hands.

And now our first baby will grow up here. If Harlow likes it, anyway.

Judging by the way her breath hitches, her ass rubbing against my lap… she likes it, alright.

"Whatever you want," I murmur against her throat. She shivers when I lick her, so salty and sweet. "Whatever you want, honey. I'll make it happen."

And I will. She's my miracle, after all.

I squeeze her thighs; thrust up against her.

A home. A baby. Anything she wants.

For the rest of our lives.

Author's Note

Thanks for reading the Wild Obsession collection! I really hope you enjoyed it.

Mountain cabins. Ocean waves. Desert dunes. I *love* the wilderness, and I loved writing these stories too.

For another instalove box set, check out the Seeing Double collection! These twin swap stories are hot, sweet, and super OTT.

Happy reading!

Cassie xxx

Cassie Mint

About the Author

Cassie writes outrageous, OTT instalove with tons of sugar and spice. She loves cookie dough, summer barbecues, and her gorgeous cat Missy.

You can connect with me on:

🌐 https://www.authorcassiemint.com

🔗 https://www.bookbub.com/authors/cassie-mint

🔗 https://www.amazon.com/~/e/B08VF8BPWG

Subscribe to my newsletter:

✉ https://www.authorcassiemint.com/newsletter